The Changes
THE WEATHERMONGER

The Changes Trilogy

The Weathermonger
Heartsease
The Devil's Children

PETER DICKINSON

The Changes
THE WEATHERMONGER

An imprint of HarperCollins_Publishers_

First published in Great Britain by Victor Gollancz 1968
Published by CollinsVoyager 2003
CollinsVoyager is an imprint of HarperCollins*Publishers* Ltd,
77-85 Fulham Palace Road, Hammersmith,
London W6 8JB

The HarperCollins website address is:
www.**fire**and**water**.com

Text © Peter Dickinson 1968, 1986

ISBN 978-0-00-714031-2

Peter Dickinson asserts the moral right to
be identified as the author of the work.

Five Years Ago...

The tunnel is dark and clammy, raw earth crudely propped. Bent double under its low roof an elderly man jabs with his crowbar at the workface, levers loose earth away, rests panting for several heartbeats and then jabs again. This time the crowbar strikes a hard surface just below the earth. He mutters and tries again, jabbing in different places, only to find each time the same smooth hardness blocking his path, sloping upwards away from him. Wearily he fetches a camper's gas lamp and peers at the obstacle, picking loose earth away from it with shaking fingers and muttering to himself all the time. Suddenly he bends closer, pursing his lips, and runs a torn thumbnail down a crack in the smooth surface. The crack goes straight as a ruler and meets the edge of the slab at an exact right angle. It is not natural rock, but stone measured and cut by masons.

His heart, which a moment before had been thudding with exhaustion, is now thudding with excitement. But he is a tidy-minded man and works methodically to clear a whole slab, and then to find leverage under it for his crowbar. Several hours pass, but at last he settles the steel into a crevice and leans his weight on it. The stone groans as it lifts. The man has a pebble ready to wedge the slit open. As he steps back to rest from that first effort he knocks his lamp over. In the new dark he sees that the slit is glowing with a pale, faint light, like a watch dial.

Something else. He does not see it, but feels it. Beyond the stone slab a Power lies.

So the Changes begin.

In that one night, all over Britain, the link between Man and Machine snapped.

On roads and motorways drivers forgot their skill and sat helpless while their cars or trucks hurtled off the tarmac. In factories the night shifts rioted and smashed. At Port Talbot a freak storm gathered and raged above the steelworks until the lightning made the whole huge complex a destroying furnace. In ordinary houses, as dawn came on, the alarm clocks rang and sleepers woke to stare at the horrible thing clanging beside them. Some hands, out of sheer muscular habit, reached out for the lightswitch, only to snatch themselves back as though the touch of plastic stung like acid.

Day after day followed of panic and rumour. Cities began to burn, amid looting and riot. Then the main flights started, hundreds of thousands of people streaming away from their homes to look for food, safety, peace. Britain closed in on itself, like an anemone in a rock pool closing at a touch. When other nations tried to probe into the island, the island seemed to grow a mysterious wall around it. It was very difficult to get even a single spy through.

But behind the wall we began to change. The Changes were mostly inside us, in our minds, but a few were outside. In a bare hill valley a great oakwood grew, overnight, with a tower in the middle of it. In Surrey a wild preacher, ranting at the roadside to the fleeing crowds, discovered that he'd called down a thunderstorm by his curses. He had willed it into being, and now he could will any weather he chose. He didn't know how, nor did the others (a boy in Weymouth, a schoolmaster in Norwich, for instance) who found they had the same gift. In a year or two it was just commonplace that there would be sun for harvest and snow in December, accepted by everyone in much the same way that they accepted that a chestnut tree would grow its five-fingered leaves every spring.

So for five white Decembers, five green springs...

It is odd how sometimes we can sense things drawing to a close – a piece of unfamiliar music, a child's tantrum, a period in our own lives. Up and down Britain people had felt the same, sensing it dimly and in fear. A housewife making tallow candles might look up from the slow and smelly job and sigh, suddenly remembering how once in that very same room she'd been able to summon good, bright lights at the touch of a switch. And then she would shudder, no longer from horror of the thing itself, but from fear that she had thought of it. If anybody should find out! She dared not even tell her husband, though he perhaps would come in that evening from his backbreaking labour at the saw pit with his own mind full of the secret memory of how quickly and accurately the big circular saws used to slice the tree trunks into planking.

People like these were warned by the fate of anyone who tried to anticipate the end – that obstinate old ship's engineer in Weymouth, for instance, who converted an old mill on the river to weave coarse cloth. All Dorset knew what the weavers did to him.

And the power that had caused the Changes still was strong. It came in pulses. There were places, too, especially in old forests, where it seemed always strong. And strong or weak it was there; on certain days the weathermongers might sense that they would need to put forth more of their mysterious gift to summon the wind or draw the molecules of water vapour into a rain cloud; but they could still do it.

But the end was coming. Unconsciously the island waited for it. But what kind of an end? A peaceful accounting of gains and losses? Or time of worse ruin even than the beginning, as the power that had been woken by the man in the tunnel threshed to and fro in its last delirious convulsions?

Contents

1

The Island

He woke up suddenly, as if from a deep sleep full of unrecoverable dreams. He was very uncomfortable. The light was too bright, even through closed eyes, and there was something sharp and hard jutting into one of his shoulder blades. His head hurt too.

He moved his right arm in search of something familiar, a sheet or a wall, and found a quite different feeling – hundreds of rough, scratchy lumps on a warm but slimy surface, like iron pimples. Familiar, though – barnacles on a sea rock. He was lying on a rock. He opened his eyes and sat up.

His skull yelped with pain as he did so, and his hand

moved instinctively to touch the smooth round thing that should have been hanging round his neck, and wasn't.

A voice beside him said, "They took it away. They hit you on the head and took it away, so that you wouldn't be able to use it."

She was a girl, about twelve, a kid with pigtails, very dirty, her face blubbered with crying, but wearing what looked like an expensive dress of green brocade with gold trimmings that would have come right down to her ankles if she'd stood up. She was sitting beside him, her knees under her chin. Beyond her the sea lay flat as a Formica tabletop, hard blue, joggling in one patch by a sunken rock just enough to catch a few glints of the vertical noon sun. A perfect day.

"Who took it?" said Geoffrey, not even remembering what "it" was.

"They did."

Without looking round she jerked her chin over her shoulder and he turned. He was on a tiny rock island, which shouldn't have been there, in the middle of Weymouth Bay. The pretty doll's houses ranged right and left along the Front above the crowded beach, and George IV's great gilt statue stood pompous at the far end. The pier was gone though, with only a few tarred and tilted timbers to show where it had been, and the crowd wasn't a holiday crowd either. They were all standing, shoulder to shoulder, looking out to sea, and all fully dressed. There wasn't a bathing suit anywhere. As he turned they roared, a long jeering moo. They were looking at him.

"What on earth are they up to?" he said.

"They're waiting for us to drown. When the tide comes in."

"Well, don't let's wait for them. It's still quite shallow. Come on."

"They won't let you ashore, but they want you to try. That's what they like. I've seen it."

"Oh, piffle! Come on."

Without waiting to see whether the girl would follow, Geoffrey hitched up his robes and stepped into the sea. A pleased hum throbbed through the crowd, like the purr of a huge cat. The water was beautifully warm; it must have been a first-rate summer; he couldn't remember. He sploshed towards the shore, hampered by his silly dressing-gown of a robe, worried about spoiling its precious gold fabric with salt water, but comforted by the real, everyday feel of watery sand under his feet. As he waded the front row of the crowd opposite where he stood looped forward into the fringe of the sea. They were all men, rather small men, but carrying what looked like spears. The whole of Weymouth Bay seemed to have shrunk a bit.

Once they had worked out where he was aiming for, the spearmen bunched there in a close line and lowered their spears. They weren't only small – they were oddly dressed, with a history-book look about them. Most of them had ordinary jackets, very patched, but some were wearing criss-cross leggings and others a sort of sacking kilt, and they all had beards. When he was a couple of feet from the spear points, which looked dead sharp, he stopped. The crowd was still as an empty beach.

"What on earth do you think you're doing?" he said to the man directly in front of him. "Come off it."

It felt odd to be talking to a grown-up like that, but there were really behaving a bit daft, and anyway he was quite as big as they were. His voice came out round and firm, without that dratted squeak.

The man (he was bald, with a coppery beard, his face tanned dark as a gipsy's, with a mesh of tiny crimson veins running under the tan on his bulgy nose) said nothing, but the line of spearmen moved another pace into the water, and the man's spear touched Geoffrey's robe, pierced it, pricked his skin. Quite right, the points *were* sharp, so it hardly hurt at all. Geoffrey stood his ground.

With a happy grin the man prodded the steel a quick half-inch further in and twisted. That hurt like mad. Geoffrey forgot his robe and the water and tried to jump back, but tripped and sat down in the clammy wetness. The crowd bayed and cheered. Geoffrey scrambled up from his defenceless sprawling, but the man made no further attack. He just stood, watching and grinning. Geoffrey looked down at the gold robe, where the blood was beginning to make its own pattern among the threads; he felt the tears of pain and defeat fat in his eyes, and (so that the crowd on the beach shouldn't see them) turned and waded back to the tiny rock island that shouldn't have been there.

As he was climbing on to it, he saw that it was really a platform made of broken slabs of concrete roughly heaped together – a platform for drowning people from. The girl had been crying again, but had stopped.

"I told you so," she said. She sounded not smug but sympathetic and miserable. Geoffrey stared at her, wondering who she was and what the people on the beach could be up to, trying to drown a couple of kids. He felt again at his chest, where the round, smooth whatever-it-was should have been, dangling from its gold chain.

"They took it away," she said. "I told you. Can't you remember *anything*?"

"Not much."

"Don't you even know who *I* am?"

"I'm afraid not."

She started to snivel again.

"I'm Sally," she said between gulpings, "your sister Sally."

Oh, Lord! Geoffrey sat down on the concrete and stared out to sea. The water had only a couple of inches to come and it would cover their island. And somewhere he'd lost five years. No wonder the Bay was smaller and people were smaller. But why had they all gone mad? He'd have to do something for Sally now, anyway, even if she was a different Sally and not the cocky six-year-old clown he knew.

"Why do they want to drown us?"

"For witches. They came to ask you about making weather and found you putting a bit of machinery from the boat into the oven. Then they banged you on the head and took your talisman away, and then they rummaged round the house and found my pictures, so they rang the church bells and brought us down here to drown."

"Making weather?"

"Yes. You did it with your talisman. You're the weathermonger in Weymouth. Every town has one. *I* think that's really why they want to drown you, because you're one of the richest men in Weymouth and they want your money. They paid you pounds and pounds for a good harvest."

"But *Quern's* still there?"

"Oh, yes, that's where the bit of engine came from which told them you were a witch. You sneak down and fiddle with her almost every week. I've seen you out of my bedroom window, though what use she is without sails *I* don't know."

"What would happen if we tried to swim round to her?"

"They'd run along and get into boats and prod you in the water. We saw a man try it last Whitsun. I laughed and laughed. Oh dear."

She started off on her gulping again. Geoffrey stared glumly at the rising water. Only half an inch to go now.

"Look," he said, "I think our best bet's to wait until the tide's right in and try and float round with our noses just out of the water and perhaps they'll think we've drowned."

"But I can't swim. I'm not a witch. I've never touched an engine since the Changes came. I only drew pictures."

Blast. Geoffrey thought he might possibly be able to swim round to the harbour undetected. It's surprising how little you can see from the shore of something that's barely moving and barely projecting from the water. But he couldn't do it if he had to lifesave Sally all the way.

"Fat chance of our getting it this weather," he said, "but what we want is a good old sea fog."

A breathing out of the water. No wind that you could feel, and nothing you could see, if you looked at any particular patch of sea. But all along the coast, from Bournemouth to Exeter, the water breathing up and being condensed into a million million million droplets in the cold layers of air above the oily surface. Cold out of the lower deeps. An un-numberable army of drops, which even the almighty sun could not feel through, breeding more layers of cold in which more armies of drops could be breathed out. And now the wind you could not feel, pushing the fog from the South, piling it up in heavy swathes against the seaward hills, thick, grey, cold. Thicker. Greyer. Colder. Thicker. Greyer. Thicker...

Sally was shaking him by the shoulder. He was sitting in six inches of water and could see about a yard through the greyness. There were shoutings from the shore, a noise of contradictory orders being given in many voices.

"I think they're getting boats and coming to throw us in," said Sally. "You could swim now. It didn't matter their taking it away after all. D'you think you can take me with you?"

Geoffrey stood up and took off his sopping robe. He folded the expensive cloth carefully and tied it in a roll with the belt, with a loop which he put round his neck so that the roll lay on his chest, where the whatever-it-was should have been. He stepped down into the deep water, on the far side of the island. It came up to his neck.

"I don't know if we'll be able to find our way in this," he whispered, "but it's better than being drowned a-purpose, like a kitten. You lie on your back and I'll hold you under your arms and pull you round. Take off your dress, though, and do it like my robe. Fine. Good girl. Off we go. Try to breathe so you've got as much air as possible in your lungs all the time. It helps you float. And pinch my leg if you hear anything that sounds like a boat."

There was no trouble finding the way in the fog. It was *his* fog, after all – he'd made it and knew, if he cared to think about it, how its tentacles reached up into the chalk valleys behind the town and its heart drifted in slow swirls above the obliterated beach. But he thought about it as little as he could, for fear of getting lost in it, mind-lost, again. He lay on his back and gave slow, rhythmic frog-kicks out to sea. He hoped it wouldn't be too smelly when they went through the patch by the outflow from the town sewer, where the best mackerel always were. Sally lay very still, like a girl already drowned.

He was beginning to worry about her, to think of risking a few words, when he felt her hand moving over his skin. She pinched him hard and he stopped kicking, slowing to a barely moving paddle. She was right. There was a squeaking of wood on wood in the greyness, between them and the beach, and it was coming nearer.

A voice said, "What's that, over there?" Pause. More squeaking. Another voice said, "Lump o' timber. This is right useless. Let's be goin' in. Who'd have thought the young wickeder would have had another talisman?" Another voice said "We'll be lucky if Dorset sees a morsel of dry hay this summer. Never cross a weathermonger, I always say. *And* he was a good un, for a young un." "He was an evil witch," said a more educated voice, fiercely. "Thou shalt not suffer a witch to live." The voices wrangled away into silence.

Geoffrey kicked on. He seemed to have been doing it for hours, and his legs were flabby after their rest. He began to count kicks, in order to keep going. Seven, eight, nine, eighty, one, two, three, four... the water was greasy with electricity under the greyness. They disturbed a gull which rose effortlessly from the surface and vanished. There didn't seem to be any smell where the sewer came out – perhaps they weren't using it any more... eight, nine, six hundred, one, two... nine, a thousand, one, two... round the corner and into the straight. Not all that far now. There was a heeling black side of the old Jersey ferry. Lord, she was rusty. Ouch!

He'd banged his head against something – a dinghy. The varnished planks seemed like a welcome home to a world he knew, after all that wet and greyness.

"Hang on here," he whispered, showing Sally where to clutch the gunwale. "Don't try to climb in."

He worked his way round to the stern, gave a final kick and heaved himself over, barking his belly a little. His legs felt empty and boneless, like one of those toy animals with zippers that women keep nighties in. Or used to, anyway. Heaven knows what they did now. He had a struggle getting Sally in – she was near the end of her strength – but managed it with a lot more noisy splashing that he cared for. There weren't any oars in the dinghy, of course, but at least he could paddle with the footboard. He moved to the bows and hauled on the painter until a blue stern solidified in the fog. *Schehallion IV* it said – Major Arkville's boat. Well, *he* wouldn't mind lending his dinghy.

"Where's *Quern*?" he whispered.

"Further down on the other quay, but it's no use going there. You want a boat with *sails*, Jeff. This one would do. You could always make a wind."

"I'd rather have an engine."

"But you haven't got the *stuff*. They burnt it all, every drop they could find. I saw it. There was a great big poof noise, and fire everywhere. The poor old

Mayor got roasted, because he stood too near."

Geoffrey felt obstinate. She was probably right, providing he *could* make a wind (but in that case who'd steer, supposing he 'went under' like when he made the fog, if he *had* made it? And anyway, if he could sail so could they – faster, probably, and the wind would blow the fog away). But he wanted to see *Quern* again, if only for Uncle Jacob's sake. He didn't want to ask Sally about Uncle Jacob, because he knew something must have happened to him. There'd have been no question of drowning kids if Uncle Jacob had been about. He paddled clumsily away from the blue stern.

Quern was tucked right in under the quay, with a line of sailing boats lashed outside her. He tied the dinghy to the outermost and crept across the decks. The ones nearer the quay were in a very lubberly condition, but *Quern* herself seemed OK. Somebody (himself, Sally said) had been looking after her. Let's hope he'd been looking after the engine too. He lifted the hatch.

The engine was speckless, but the tank was quite empty. Geoffrey ducked into the cabin and crawled through the hatch in the forward bulkhead to where Uncle Jacob kept the spare cans ("As far from the engine as possible, laddie. Fire at sea is a terrible thing.

I've seen it."). There were three big jerry cans, all full, which had evidently been missed at the time of the Mayor-roasting. He lugged one back and rummaged for dry clothes in the port locker. Two oily jerseys, two pairs of jeans – terrific.

Sally was peering down into the engine hatch, shivering.

"It's like one of my pictures," she said.

"You'd better get into these."

"But they'll beat me if they find me wearing trousers. It isn't *womanly*."

"If they find you they'll... ach, never mind. But I can't remember whether it's womanly or not, and no one else will see you. Off you go, and I'll try and get this thing running."

She crept into the cabin, and Geoffrey bent to the engine. He filled the tank, turned the petrol switch, closed the choke, flooded the carburettor and swung the handle. It wasn't as stiff as he expected, which meant that he must have been turning it over from time to time. He swung again. Nothing. And again. And again. Nothing. He looked at the filter glass under the carburettor and found it was full of water – of course. There'd have been quite a bit of condensation in the tank. He unscrewed the glass and let the petrol flow for a little into the bilge. As he was preparing to swing again he realised that the magneto-cover was loose, and lifted it off. No magneto. No hope then. Wait a sec, though; there might be a spare. Uncle Jacob was a maniac for spares, always taking up good locker-space with things he'd be unlucky to need once in a lifetime. His cronies had said that he sailed with a complete spare ship on board.

There was a magneto in the big locker in the cabin, sealed in a polythene bag. Sally gasped when she saw it.

"Jeff, that's what you were putting in the oven when they came and banged you on the head. Really they'd only come to ask for a night shower. Did you know?"

"In the oven?"

Oh, yes, of course. If he'd been looking after the boat he'd have taken the magneto up from time to time to dry it out. Bad luck to be caught with it. He adjusted the spare, clipped the cover into place, and swung the engine again. It coughed, died, coughed again and caught – though it didn't sound too happy. He opened the choke a little, adjusted the engine to idle, climbed the iron rungs to the quay and cast off every rope he could see. There was a babble of shouts from the direction of the town. A window slammed up above his head and a woman, screeching, began to throw candlesticks at him. He jumped down into the cockpit, put the throttle hard down and the gear to forward, and swung the wheel to port. The whole raft of boats started to move. There was open water between them and the quay. A noise of boots running on cobbles came through the fog. The locked boats wheeled out into the harbour, slowly, slowly. There was a four-foot, a five-foot gap now, with the black harbour water plopping muddily against weedy timbers. A man, a bearded man in a knitted cap, jumped with a grunt on to the deck, but only just made it. As he stood teetering with his knees against the rail, Sally charged yelling out of the cabin and butted her head into his stomach. He went over backwards, arms windmilling, with a luscious splash. Now they were in the middle of the harbour, safe until boats could be got out.

Geoffrey, one hand still on the wheel, throttled down, put the gear to neutral and felt in the fire-fighting locker for the hatchet. Still there. He ran along the deck, hacking through the painters that lashed them to the other boats. The last ropes parted with a slap and twang. Back in the cockpit he revved up and put the gear to forward. Free after five years' idleness, *Quern* danced away down the harbour (a rather sick dancer).

"Well done, Sal."

She laughed, and he recognised at last the six-year-old he'd known.

2

THE CHANNEL

Twenty minutes later they came out of the fog: a soft south wind was putting a tiny lop on to the water, making it flash, million-faceted, under the sun. It heaved sleepily too, stirred by the slow remains of Atlantic rollers. England, behind them, was still lost in greyness.

Geoffrey went into the cabin and found his gold robe. The salt-water stains were leaving it mottled and blobbed, but it was still too damp to show how bad the final result would be. He took it out to spread on the cabin roof. Coming out, he noticed how much sicker the engine was sounding than when he'd started, and realised at the same time how much the spear-prick in his chest was beginning to hurt. The first-aid box was in its proper locker. ("Never stint yourself for splints and bandages, laddie. I've seen men die for want of a proper dressing.")

"What happened to Uncle Jacob, Sal?"

"The weavers killed him. They came from all over Dorset and threw stones at him, and the neighbours watched out of their windows. It was because of something he was trying to do in the big shed by the stream. Shall I help you with that?"

She wasn't much help, not knowing how Elastoplast worked, but he managed quite a neat patch, with some analgesic cream (rather thick and crumbly with age) on the actual cut. Then he decided he ought to do something about the engine, or try to. He'd watched Uncle Jacob tinkering often enough, and done simple jobs himself, but he knew that it would have to be something pretty easy and obvious if he was going to tackle it alone. At least the tools would be there. ("No use trying to do a complicated job with a knife and fork, laddie. I've seen ships lost at sea for the lack of the right wrench.") He put the engine into neutral and stopped it. When he opened the hatch a blast of scorching air weltered up at him and there was a guggle of boiling water in the cooling system.

Oil? He'd been so cock-a-hoop about finding the petrol that he'd forgotten to check the oil. Just like him to get this far and then land himself, by sheer stupidity, with a hopelessly buckled crankshaft. But the dipstick, too hot to hold without a cloth, showed reasonably clean oil up to the "Full" mark, though it smoked bluely and gave off a bitter smell of burning.

Cooling system then? Yes. There was far more water in the bilge than there should have been, and both hoses were dripping and hissing. He took off his jersey and bent down to try the intake hose. Damn! His arm seemed to come back of its own accord, like a recoiling snake, five inches of skin scorched white by the quivering metal. He rubbed in Antical and tried again more carefully. Both hoses were perished, useless.

"Is there anything for me to do, Jeff?"

"I don't think so. Wait a sec while I look at the spare hose."

There was a decent length of it in the locker, but this too was mostly cracked and powdery. He needed about eight good inches for the intake: the outlet could take care of itself, really, provided they didn't mind a bit of bailing. One stretch in the middle of the spare felt not too bad, and while he was reaching down to measure it against the rotten piece his eye was caught by the filter-bowl under the carburettor. It was dark with little crumbly bits of brown stuff, like coffee grounds – rust off the inside of the jerry cans. Much more of that and the jet would be choked. He went into the cabin and found two plastic buckets and a plastic sieve.

"Look, Sal, if you pour the petrol out of this can into those buckets through this strainer, all but a little bit, you can give the last drops a good swill round and empty it over the side. Then you can pour it back into the can through this funnel – and we'll have some clean petrol. And keep an eye on the coast. This sun will clear the fog up in a jiffy and they'll spot us."

"You could make another one."

"I dunno. I've a feeling that's all there is, by way of fog, for the moment. It takes an awful lot of cold. You can't make bricks without straw. I dare say I could make a calm."

"They've got rowing boats, and quite big ones. They go terribly fast. Do you really mean that you can't remember how you make weather?"

"I can't remember anything, Sal. It must be

something to do with being hit on the head. You'll have to explain to me what's been going on."

"The Changes, you mean? I don't know much. We weren't supposed to talk about them."

"Well, tell me what you know later. It's more important to get that petrol clean now. And keep a good look out."

He went back to the perished hose. The good bit of spare would just about do. The trouble was that to get a screwdriver into the bulldog clip at the inner end involved working with his hands slap up against the scorching cylinder block. He got a towel out of the cabin, soaked it in the sea and hung it, hissing, down the side of the engine. The screw was very stiff, and before he got it to move the towel was dry and turning toast-brown in places. He soaked it again, and this time moved the screw a quarter-turn before he had to damp the cloth again. Three more goes and it was loose. The other end ought to be easy.

"Jeff, there are boats putting out."

She was right; he could see half a dozen water beetles, just outside the mole, scratches on the surface of the blue-glass sea.

"OK, Sal, I'll see what I can do. When you've

finished that you might see if you can do something about the outlet hose – this thing here. I haven't got enough spare to change it, but if you cut a piece out of one of the sou'westers in the cabin – there ought to be scissors in the galley drawer – you could bind that round and round with insulating tape – here – as tight as you can. Several layers, and then it shouldn't do more than drip. I don't know how long I'll be."

He hadn't put his jersey back on, so the robe lay next to his skin. The gold threads were fat with the warmth of the sun. All round the Channel basked, like a sleeping animal, and on its skin the beetles moved towards them, murderous. They were larger now. He sat on the roof of the cabin with his chin on his knees, judging his time.

Now.

A squall, from the south-west. Airs gathered over the Atlantic, moving steadily eastward under the massaging of the high stratospheric gales, in their turn moved by the turning world, dangling behind it like streamers. The march of airs flawed and splintered on meeting the land mass of Europe, some sucked back in whirlpools, some shoved on in random eddies, funnelled by invisible pressures. One here, now, crumpling the water, a fist of

wind, tight, hard, cold, smashing north-east, hurling a
puny fleet of beetles about in a pother of waters and
broken oars and cries that carried for miles, then on,
inland across the unyielding oaks of the New Forest, to
shiver into eddies and die out among the Downs.

When he came to, Sally was making a neat finish to
the outlet hose. She had bandaged it over and over, like
the broken leg of a doll. She smelt of petrol and looked
sad.

"I hope there wasn't anyone we know," she said.
"You broke two of the boats, and the other four picked
a lot of people out of the water and they all went
home."

"Fine."

"Look, Jeff, I found this in the cupboard where you
got the tape from. I didn't know you had another one."

"That's an ammeter. You use it for measuring electric
currents. What do you mean, another one?"

"Oh, *but...* oh Jeff, it was your talisman – the thing
they took away when they hit you on the head. They
thought you couldn't make weather without it. You
wore the other one on a gold chain round your neck,
and you *hit* me once when I touched it. You're much
nicer, now, since they tried to drown you, you know."

"I'm sorry, Sal."

Funny, he thought. Perhaps if you have powers that seem magical you are a bit frightened of them, and so you have to pretend to yourself that the magic isn't in you but in something that belongs to you, a talisman. He still felt like that – superstitious, so to speak – about the gold robe. It would be interesting to try and make weather, something easy like a frosty night, without even that. Not now, though. He took the robe off and lay on the deck planks to detach the outer end of the hose and fit the new piece. The cylinder block was cool enough to touch now.

"Tell me about the Changes, Sal."

"I really don't know very much. They happened when I was a little girl. Everyone suddenly started hating machines and engines. No, not everyone. A lot of people went away, over the sea. They just started feeling miserable in England, I think. There are whole towns quite empty, or that's what they say. And after that anyone who used a machine, or even anyone who just seemed to like machines, they called a witch. And I think everyone started to become more and more old-fashioned, too. Really, that's all I know. I'm terribly hungry; aren't you?"

"Yes, I am. Famished. Go and see if there's any gas in the butane cylinders. I saw some tins in the larder. You could rustle up some grub while I finish this lot off."

"I'm afraid you'll have to show me how."

The butane hissed happily, but most of the matches in the larder were duds. Geoffrey worked almost through a whole box before he got a light, and then he panicked and dropped the match. The second box was better, and he got the cooker going. There was fresh water in the tank, quite sweet, which was another sign of how carefully he'd been servicing *Quern* in his forgotten-dream world. He had to show Sally how to put a saucepan on and how to open a tin. Then he went back to his engine. It took him half an hour to fit the hose and clear the carburettor jet, and when he turned the crank it moved quite easily. He must have stopped the engine just in time, before the heat could do any real damage. It started at once when he turned the petrol on and swung it again; it sounded fine now. He swung *Quern*'s head south. France seemed the best bet. He thought about all the people who had left England – there must have been thousands, millions of them, unable to live in a world without machines. How'd they got out? How many had died? Where had they gone?

He locked the wheel, after five minutes' pointless guessing, and went in to see what sort of a mess Sally had made of supper. It was beef stew and butter beans, and it was delicious. They ate it out in the cockpit, with the engine churning smoothly and the first stars showing.

"Is France the right place to go, Sal? We could turn round and land somewhere else on the English coast, where they don't know us."

"We couldn't land in this. They'd kill us at once. France is where all the others went, Uncle Jacob said. When he found out about me drawing pictures he wanted us all to go there, but you wouldn't. You liked being one of the richest men in Weymouth too much."

"I'm sorry."

"Anyway, we're going to France now."

"OK. I'll go and see what charts we've got. I wonder if we've got enough fuel to go all the way to Morlaix."

There was a message in the middle of the big Channel chart, written in Uncle Jacob's backward-sloping hand on a folded piece of tissue paper. It said:

Good luck, laddie. I should have taken you and Sal south long ago, before you got hooked on this weather thing. Now I don't think I shall last long. I'm going to try and wean these fools of burghers from their cottage industries by building them a water-driven power loom. Can't be much harm in that, but you never know. This anti-machine thing seems a bit erratic in its effects — it's pretty well worn off me now, but it seems just as strong as ever with most of the honest citizens of Weymouth. I can't be the only one. It's not sense. But everyone's too afraid even to drop a hint to his neighbour (me too). We'll just have to see what happens.

One thing I'd like to do is go nosing about up on the Welsh borders, Radnor way. There's talk about that being where the whole thing is coming from.

You'll find a spot of cash in Cap'n Morgan's hidey-hole.

Geoffrey went and looked in the secret drawer under his old bunk. If you felt under the mattress there was a little hook which you pulled, and that undid the catch and you could push the panel in. Uncle Jacob had made it for him to keep his spare Crunchie bars in, but now all it held was a soft leather purse containing thirty gold sovereigns. In a fit of rage he thought of the men he'd spilt into the roaring sea with his squall, and hoped that some of the people who had stoned Uncle Jacob had been among them. Then he thought about that last trip to Brittany, in the summer hols when he was ten, and decided to go to Morlaix if they possibly could. He did some sums and realised it would be a close thing: but he needn't make up his mind until they were on their last can of petrol.

"Time you turned in, Sal. One of us ought to be awake all the time, just in case. I'll give you four hours' sleep, and then you can come and be Captain while I have a snooze."

When the time came to wake her he couldn't, she was so deep under. And he was tired all through, so that unconsidered nooks of his body screamed at him for sleep. He cut the engine, turned off the petrol and rolled into his bunk, wondering whether a night's dreaming would bring back his memory of the lost six years.

3

The General

A noise like the end of the world woke him. The room was bucketing about. His first thought was earthquake! Then the noise came again as the two tins from last night's supper rattled across the floor, and he remembered he was on *Quern*. She was rocking wildly. He ran out on deck and saw a big steamer belting eastward, trailing the ridged wake that was tossing them about. Sally came out too, still almost asleep, staggering and bumping into things. She blinked at the liner and put her thumb in her mouth. It was just after eight, supposing he'd set the clock right the night before. He started the engine and went to look for some breakfast.

Supper out of tins can be fine, but not breakfast. They ate ham and spaghetti.

They saw a few more ships on the way over, and about mid-morning the first of the big jets whined over them. Sally put her thumb in her mouth again and said nothing. Geoffrey realised that the previous afternoon they hadn't seen a single proper ship or aeroplane in all their twenty-mile circle of visibility.

It was about four, and raining, when they chugged up the listless waters of Morlaix estuary and made fast to the quay, with a cupful of petrol left in the tank. An absurd train, a diesel, hooted as it crossed the prodigious viaduct that spans the valley where old Morlaix lies. Sally cried out when she saw it.

"Oh, that's another of my pictures?"

There were proper cars slamming along the roads on either side of the mooring basin. She stared at them, and her thumb crept to her mouth yet again.

"Don't they go fast?" she said. "Why don't they hit each other? They look awfully dangerous. And they smell."

Yes, they *did* smell. Geoffrey hadn't remembered that. Or perhaps five years in a land without exhaust fumes had sharpened his senses. There was a very

French-looking boy fishing wetly in the corner of the basin. Geoffrey dredged in his mind for scraps of language.

"Nous sommes Anglais," he said, shy with the certainty that he wouldn't be able to manage much more.

"Oh, are you?" said the boy. "So'm I. You mean you've only just come over? I say, you *are* late." He gave a short laugh, as if at a joke he didn't expect anyone else to see. "I'll take you along to the office, though it's probably shut – practically no one comes over any more. Monsieur Pallieu will be tickled pink to have a bit of work to do."

The office was upstairs in a harsh but handsome building close to the quay. It said DEPARTMENT DES IMMIGRES on the door. There were voices inside.

"You're in luck," said the boy. "He's probably brought some crony back from lunch to help him swill Pernod."

He tapped on the door and lounged in without waiting for an answer, as though it were his own house. From behind they saw a ludicrous change come over his demeanour, as he clutched off his dripping beret and jerked his insolent slouch into respectful attention. He spoke politely.

"I've brought two new immigrés to see you, Monsieur Pallieu. They're kids."

"Diable!" said one voice.

"Thank you, Ralph," said another. "Let them come in."

The room was extremely hot, and smelt of dust, paper, gasfire, wet umbrellas and people. There were two men in it, a small grey gentleman who didn't look like anyone in particular and introduced himself as M. Pallieu; and a larger man in an untidy tweed jacket who looked distinctly like somebody – he had a square, tanned face, close-cut black hair above it, and a bristling little moustache in the middle of it. M. Pallieu said he was General Turville, Inspecteur du Département. The two were sitting behind a desk which was covered with neat piles of paper, all containing rows of figures.

The General muttered in French to M. Pallieu, and went over to stare out of the window at the rain. M. Pallieu fetched two chairs for the children.

"Please sit down," he said. "The General has kindly consented to wait while I take your particulars. We were, in fact, discussing the possibility of closing this office down, so you have arrived in the nick. Now," he reached for a form, "names, please."

"Geoffrey and Sally Tinker."

"Your ages?"

Geoffrey looked at Sally.

"I'm eleven and he's sixteen," she said.

"Do you not know your own age, young man?" said M. Pallieu.

"They hit me on the head yesterday," said Geoffrey, "and something seems to have gone wrong with my memory."

"Ah." M. Pallieu didn't seem at all surprised, but went on asking questions in his beautiful English and filling in the form. He had nearly finished when he said, "Do you possess any money?"

"I've got thirty gold sovereigns, and I suppose we could sell the boat if we had to."

"You came in your own boat? It is not stolen?"

"No. It belonged to my Uncle Jacob, but he's dead, and Sally is sure he left it to me."

"Ce bâteau là?" the General barked from the window, so odd and abrupt a sound that at first Geoffrey thought he was only clearing his throat.

"Yes, that's her. She's called *Quern.*"

The General jerked his head at M. Pallieu, who went across the room and looked out of the window. He sounded a little less kindly when he turned back and spoke again.

"Let us have this clear. You claim to have come from Weymouth in that white motor boat we can all see down there?"

"Yes," said Geoffrey. "Why?"

"He doesn't think we could have done it in a *motor* boat," said Sally.

"Exactly," said M. Pallieu. "Furthermore, it is well known that the Government of France is extremely interested to meet *immigrés* upon whom the English scene does not appear to produce its customary symptoms, and there have been a number of impostors who have made this claim. They expected to be given money."

"Did they come in motor boats?" asked Geoffrey.

"Of course. That appeared to substantiate their claim."

"Oh dear," said Sally.

"On the other hand," said M. Pallieu, "they were not children. Nor did many of them have as much as thirty gold sovereigns. With the General's permission, we had better hear your story and then we can perhaps judge."

"They were trying to drown us for being witches," said Sally, "but Jeff made a fog and swam me round to the harbour and found some of the stuff you put in the engine to make it go and I pushed a man overboard and we got out of the harbour and then the engine stopped and the fog went away and the men came after us in boats and Jeff made a wind and abolished them and mended the engine and I helped him and then I made supper on a sort of oven that went *whish* with blue fire which came out of a bottle and here we are."

"Let us take it more slowly," said M. Pallieu.

He asked questions for what seemed hours. Sally had to do most of the answering. The General leaned over the desk and barked occasionally. They kept coming back to the starting of the engine in the harbour and the mending of it out at sea. At one point the General himself tramped down to *Quern* and nosed around. He came back with some odd things, including a mildewy burgee and a packet of very mouldy biscuits. At last they had a low-voiced talk in French. Then M. Pallieu turned to the children.

"Well," he said, "we think that either you are telling the truth or that some adult has arranged an extra-ordinarily thorough piece of deception and used you as a bait. Even so, how would he obtain five-year-old English gingernuts? So, really, we do not think you are impostors, but we wish there was some way of proving your story. There are many things about it that are most important – this business about making weather, for instance. That would explain much."

"Would it help if Jeff stopped the rain?" said Sally.

The two men looked at him, and he realised he would have to try. He reached up under his jersey, under his left arm, and pulled out the rolled robe. He unrolled it and hung it over the back of the chair while he took his jersey off. Then he put the robe on. Odd how familiar the silly garment felt, as a knight's armour must, or a surgeon's mask, something they'd worn as a piece of professional equipment every time they did their job. He opened the casement and leaned his hand on the sill, staring at the sky. He did not feel sure he could do it; the power in him seemed weak, like a radio signal coming from very far away. He felt for the clouds with his mind.

From above they were silver, and the sun trampled on them, ramming his gold heels uselessly into their clotting softness. But there were frail places in the fabric. Push now, sun here, at this weakness, ram through with

47

a gold column, warming the under-air, hammering it hard, as a smith hammers silver. Turn now, air, in a slow spiral, widening, a spring of summer, warmth drawing in more air as the thermal rises to push the clouds apart, letting in more sun to warm the under-air. Now the fields steam, and in the clouds there is a turning lake of blue, a turning sea, spinning the rain away. More sun...

"He always goes like that," said Sally. "We never knew when to wake him."

In the streets the humps of the cobbles were already dry, and the lines of water between them shone in the early evening light. The café proprietor on the far side of the basin was pulling down a blue and red striped awning with CINZANO written on it.

The General was using the telephone, forcing his fierce personality along the wires to bully disbelieving clerks at the far end. At last he seemed to get the man he wanted, changed his tone and listened for a full two minutes. Then he barked "Merci bien" and put the receiver down. He turned and stared at the children.

"Vous ne parlez pas Français?" he said.

"Un peu," said Geoffrey, "mais..." The language ran into the sand.

"And I too the English," said the General. "How they did teach us badly! Monsieur Pallieu will speak, and I will essay to comprehend."

"The General," said M. Pallieu, "has been speaking to the meteorological office at Paris. We wished to know whether this break in the clouds was just coincidence. After all, you might have felt a change coming, and risked it. But, apparently, he is satisfied that you, Mr Tinker, did the trick yourself. Now, you must understand that the only phenomenon we have actually been able to observe over England during the last five years has been the weather. Most western powers – France, America, Russia, Germany – have sent agents in to your island, but very few have returned. Some, we think, were killed, and some simply decided to stay: 'went native', you might say. Those who did return brought no useful information, except that the island was now fragmented into a series of rural communities, united by a common hostility to machines of any sort, and by a tendency to try to return to the modes of living and thought that characterised the Dark Ages. The agents themselves say that they felt similar urges, and were tempted to stay too.

"Of course, at first we tried to send aeroplanes over,

but the pilots, without exception, lost confidence in their ability to fly their machines before they were across the coast. Some managed to turn back but most crashed. Then we tried with pilotless planes; these penetrated further, but were met before long with freak weather conditions of such ferocity that they were broken into fragments.

"Despite these warnings, a number of English exiles formed a small army, backed financially by unscrupulous interests, and attempted an invasion. They said that the whole thing was a communist plot, and that the people of England would rally to the banner of freedom. Of the three thousand who left, seven returned in two stolen boats. They told a story of mystery and horror, of ammunition that exploded without cause, of strange monsters in the woods, of fierce battles between troops who were all parts of the same unit, of a hundred men charging spontaneously over a cliff, and so on. Since then we have left England alone.

"Except for the satellites. These, it seems, move too high and too fast to be affected by the English phenomenon, and from them we can at least photograph the weather patterns above the island. They are very strange. For centuries, the English climate has been an international joke, but now you have perfect weather – endless fine summers, with rain precisely when the crops need it; deep snow every Christmas, followed by iron frosts which break up into early, balmy springs; and then the pattern is repeated. But the pattern itself is freckled with sudden patches of freak weather. There was, for instance, a small thunder area which stayed centred over Norwich for three whole weeks last autumn, while the rest of the country enjoyed ideal harvest weather. There are some extraordinary cloud-formations on the Welsh border, and up in Northumberland. But anywhere may break out into a fog, or a storm, or a patch of sun, against all meteorological probability, in just the way you brought the sun to us now.

"So you are doubly interesting to us, Mr Tinker. First, because you explain the English weather pattern. And secondly, because you appear to be genuinely immune to the machine phobia which affects anyone who sets foot in England. You seem to be the first convincing case in the twenty million people who have left England."

"Twenty million!" said Geoffrey. "How did they all get out?"

"The hour brings forth the man," said M. Pallieu, "especially if there is money involved. All one summer the steamers lay off the coast, on the invisible border where the effect begins to manifest itself, and the sailing boats plied out to them. Most had given all they possessed to leave. They came by the hundred thousand. I had twelve men working under me in Morlaix alone, and in Calais they had three whole office blocks devoted to coping with the torrent of refugees. That is what you English were, refugees. When I was your age, Mr Tinker, I saw the refugees fleeing west before Hitler's armies, carrying bedding, babies and parrots, wheeling their suitcases in barrows and prams, a weeping, defeated people. That is how they came to us, five years ago.

"And nobody knows how many have died. There can, one imagines, be no real medicine. Plague must have ravaged the cities. We know from the satellites that London and Glasgow burnt for weeks. And still we do not know what has caused this thing."

"Why does it matter so much to you?" asked Geoffrey. It was the General who answered.

"If this can arrive to England," he said, "it can arrive to France. And to Russia. And to America. Your country has a disease, boy. First we isolate, then we investigate. It is not for England we work, but for Europe, for the world, for France."

"Well," said Geoffrey, "I'll tell you everything I can, but it isn't much because I've lost my memory. And so will Sal, but I honestly don't think she knows much about what happens outside Weymouth. Really what I'd like to do is go back, if you'll help me, and try and find out – not for France or the world or anything, but just to know." (And for Uncle Jacob: and he wasn't going to tell them about Radnor, if he could help it.)

"Can I come too?" said Sally.

"No," said Geoffrey and M. Pallieu together.

"Yes, she must go," said the General.

"I don't think I like it here," said Sally. "I think those things are horrible."

She pointed out of the window at a Renault squealing ecstatically round a right-angled bend at 60 kph and accelerating away across the bridge, watched by a benign gendarme.

"You would soon be accustomed to them," said M. Pallieu.

"You'd better stay, Sal," said Geoffrey. "Honestly

England sounds much more dangerous. Nobody is going to drown you here, just for drawing pictures."

The General grunted and looked at Sally.

"You are right, mamselle, you must go," he said. "Your brother has no memory of what arrives in England today. He must have a guide, and you are the only possible. Michel, it is necessary." He spoke firmly in French to M. Pallieu, and Geoffrey, used now to the sound of French, grasped that he was saying that the children had not much to tell, but might possibly find out more than previous agents. Then he turned to Geoffrey.

"Young man, with your powers you have weapons that are stronger, in the conditions, than the anti-tank gun. If we send you to England, what will you do? You cannot explore a whole island, two hundred thousand square kilometres."

"I think I'd go and explore the freak weather centres," said Geoffrey. "That one on the Welsh borders sounds interesting."

"Why?" The General pounced on him, overbore him, wore him down with stares and grunts. In the end it seemed simplest to tell them about Uncle Jacob's message, and the gossip about the Radnor border.

"Understood," said the General. "We must direct you to that point. You will find out the location, the exact location, of the disturbance, and then we will send missiles across. We will cauterise the disease. And when you come back, you can make us some more French weather. For the last five years we have endured your horrible English weather. The rain must go somewhere, is it not, Michel?"

He laughed, a harsh yapping noise, as if he were not used to the exercise.

"Yes, General," said M. Pallieu sadly.

4

BACK

A fortnight later, in a warm dusk, they were lounging up the Solent under the wings of a mild wind from the south-west, passengers only, on a beautiful thirty-foot ketch skippered by Mr Raison, a solemn fat furniture-designer who'd been one of the first to leave England. The General had chosen him, hauled him all the way up from Nice, because he had once kept a yacht on Beaulieu River, with his own smart, teak bungalow by the shore. He had spent every weekend of his English life sailing devotedly on those waters, until he could smell his way home in a pitch-black gale.

The crew was English too. They were brothers

called Basil and Arthur. Six years before they had lived near Bournemouth, fishermen in the off season, but making most of their livelihood out of trips for tourists in the delicious summer months. Now they owned a small garage in Brest, which the General had threatened to close down unless they joined the adventure – but Geoffrey, knowing them now, realised they would have come of their own accord if they had been asked in the right way.

The ketch belonged to an angry millionaire, who hadn't been willing to lend it until he received a personal telephone call from the President of France. (His wife had put on her tiara to listen to the call on an extension.) It was the best boat anyone knew of which did not have an engine. The point was that they still knew absurdly little about the reaction of England to machines. Would the people sense the presence of a strange engine, even if it wasn't running? Would the weather gather its force to drive them back? Sally thought not, but it wasn't worth the risk.

They were going to have to rely on an engine in the end. This was the upshot of the second lot of arguments in Morlaix. (The first had been about whether Sally should come at all, Geoffrey and M. Pallieu versus Sally and the General. Sally's side had won hands down, partly because Sally really was the only one who knew what she was talking about, and partly because the General had enough willpower to beat down three Geoffreys and twenty M. Pallieus.) The problem had been how the children should move the hundred and fifty miles across England to the Welsh borders. Should they walk, and risk constant discovery in a countryside where every village (Sally said) regarded all strangers as enemies? Obviously not, if they could help it.

At first they'd assumed that any mechanical means were out of the question, and the General had scoured the country for strong but docile ponies. But the riding lessons had been a disaster: Sally was teachable, but Geoffrey was not. Five minutes astride the most manageable animal in northern France left him sore, sulky and irresponsible. They persevered for five days, at the end of which it was clear that he would never make a long journey in that fashion, though he could now actually stay in the saddle for perhaps half an hour at a time. But he obviously didn't belong there. The most dim-witted peasant in England would be bound to stare and ask questions.

It was M. Pallieu who came up with the mad,

practical idea. He pointed out that the engine of *Quern* had worked, at least. This implied that the English effect was dormant in the case of engines which had been in England all along, without running. England had got used to their presence. Would not the best thing be to find a car which had been abandoned in England and was still in working condition?

"Impossible," barked the General.

But no, argued M. Pallieu. It happened that his friend M. Salvadori, with whom he played belotte in the evenings, was a fanatic for early motorcars. Fanatics are fanatics; whatever their subject, stamps, football, trains – they know all there is to know about it. And M. Salvadori had talked constantly of this fabulous lost treasure-store, not two hundred kilometres away over the water, at Beaulieu Abbey: the Montagu Motor Museum.

When the Changes came, Lord Montagu had been among the exiles; but before he left he had 'cocooned' every car in his beloved museum, spraying them with plastic foam to preserve them from corrosion. (Navies do the same with ships they don't need.) Could they not at least attempt to steal a car from the museum, something enormously simple and robust, and dash across England until they were within range of the country they wanted to explore? M. Salvadori suggested the famous 1909 Rolls Royce Silver Ghost.

The General had sat quite still for nearly two minutes. Then he had spent two hours telephoning. Next morning a marvellous old chariot trundled into Morlaix, with a very military-looking gentleman sitting bolt upright and absurdly high behind its steering wheel, and all the urchins cheering. So Geoffrey had his first driving lessons on that queen of all cars, the Silver Ghost, taught by a man to whom driving was a formal art and not (as it is to most of us) a perfunctory achievement.

It had not been easy. In 1909 the man who drove had to be at least as clever as his car. Nowadays they build for idiots, and most cars, even the cheap ones, have to be a good deal cleverer than some of their owners. So Geoffrey, sweaty with shame, groaned and blushed as he crashed those noble gears with the huge, long-reaching lever, or stalled the impeccable, patient engine. But he improved quite quickly. Indeed, before the messenger sent by the General to Lord Montagu in Corfu returned, the military-looking gentleman went so far as to tell him that he had a certain knack with motors. The messenger had brought back sketch-plans of the Abbey and the Museum, and, best of all, keys.

So now here they were, heading up the estuary through the silken dusk, with fifty gallons of petrol in the cabin, a wheelbarrow on deck, together with the ram which Basil and Arthur had run up in their garage, and beside them two big canisters of decocooning fluid, spare tyres, two batteries, a bag of tools, cartons of sustaining food, bedding, and so on. Perhaps the most curious item of all was Sally's wallet of horse bait, in case the Rolls was a flop and they had to trudge into the New Forest and steal ponies after all. The General had dug up a professional horse-thief, a gipsy. He had been very old and smelly, and had smiled yellowly all the time, but he'd pulled out of pocket after pocket little orange cubes that smelt like celestial hay. He had whined horribly at the General for more money, but when he realised that he'd been given as much as he was going to get he had changed his personality completely, becoming easy and solemn, and had said that Sally was born to great good fortune.

They could see the banks of the estuary now, on both sides, a darker greyness between the steel-grey water and the blue-grey sky. The rich men's yachts were all gone. There was a noise of hammering and a flaring of lights from Buckler's Hard, as if the old shipyard were once again building oaken sea-goers, in a hurry after two hundred years of inanition. The banks came closer. There were houses visible by the shapes of their roofs against the skyline, but few showed any lights in a land where once again men went to bed at dusk and rose at dawn. A dog howled and Geoffrey cringed a little in the darkness, sure that the animal spoke for the whole countryside, that somehow it had sensed them and their cargo, alien and modern; sure that they would land to meet a crowd of aroused villagers, bristling with staves and spears (like the soldier-men at Weymouth) who would chump them all into shapeless bloody fragments, like the jaws of some huge, mindless hound. But no dog answered; there was no calling of voices from dark house to dark house, no sudden scurrying of lanterns; the ketch whispered on through the darkness between the black, still woods on either side of the water.

After an endless time the two brothers held a low-voiced talk with Mr Raison, crept forward and brought the mainsail down with a faint clunking. They drifted along, barely moving, under the jib. Staring forward,

Geoffrey saw the reach of water down which they were sailing darken in the distance, as if it were passing through the blackness under trees. Mr Raison gave a low whistle and put the wheel over. The jib came down, flapping twice like a shot pheasant. The anchor hissed overboard (its chains had been replaced with nylon rope at Morlaix). They were there. The ketch lay in the centre of the pool below the Abbey. The blacker patch of water had been land.

Sally pulled the trailing dinghy in by its painter and Geoffrey eased himself in, then stood, wobbling slightly, to receive stores, stowing canisters and bedding all around him until there were only three inches of freeboard left, and barely room for Basil to lower himself in and row them ashore. He really was an expert. He pulled with short, tidy strokes and caught the oars out of the water with a cupping twist of the wrists that made neither swirl nor splash. The only sound was that of a few drops from the oar-tips.

They unloaded their cargo over a patch of bank slimy with the paddling of ducks, and Basil went back for more. Geoffrey sat on a drier patch higher up the bank and stared at the star-reflecting water. The ketch was invisible against trees.

Thank heavens, anyway, he hadn't needed to make a wind for them. The breeze, which had been perfect, was now dying away to stillness, and soon there'd be an off-shore wind to take the ketch out. But they'd a good four hours' work to do before then, and four hours seemed nothing when you thought that before next nightfall Sally and he would, like as not, be dead. Funny to think of all those distinguished officers scampering across Europe, bullying underlings down the telephone, just in order to land a couple of kids in Hampshire to steal a motorcar, when the odds were that all three, the Rolls and Sally and himself, would finish up among the rusting rubbish at the bottom of a duck pond.

He began to worry again about Sally, though she'd been happy and excited on the way over. She'd hated France with its whizzing cars and jostling citizens. The only aspects of civilisation she'd really enjoyed had been Coca-Cola and ice creams, and she'd got on best with the smelly old gipsy man. After he'd left she had filled every spare nook of her clothes with the orange horse-bait, which she kept pulling out to sniff during their endless planning sessions.

Suppose that by some crazy fluke they brought it off and England became again the England he remembered, would Sally ever be happy? And then there was the General. At first Geoffrey had worshipped him, a magnificent manifestation of absolute will, whose orders you obeyed simply because he was giving them; but then he'd found himself puzzled by the great man's actual motives: the readiness to slaughter a couple of kids on the off chance of pulling off a far-fetched coup; the cheerful suggestion of blotting out half a happy county with missiles – did he really know what he was up to? Or was he like a mindless machine, pounding away towards some unthought-out purpose. Geoffrey had asked about the missiles, and what good it would do to obliterate the trouble without finding out the cause, and the General had just laughed his barking laugh and said "Shoot first, ask questions afterwards."

They were taking the devil of a time about re-loading the dinghy. Perhaps Sally was having second thoughts – be a good thing if she did, really. It was damned unfair blackmailing a kid to come on a business like this, and that went for himself, too. Why did it have to be *them*? Had the General honestly made an effort to find anyone else who was immune to the Effect, or had he just seized on their chance arrival as an opportunity to exercise his own self-justifying will? Serve the great man right if the

Rolls turned out to have been burnt by angry peasants. In that case he was certainly not going to go loping off into the dark to steal ponies – and they'd hang you now for that, Sally said – Blast! The dry patch he was sitting on wasn't as dry as he'd thought, and the cold came through the seat of his trousers like a guilty conscience. He stood up and stared at the stars, then walked up on to the road.

When the dinghy came back he was exploring the potholes in the unrepaired tarmac and wondering whether they'd brought enough spare tyres. Sally came up the bank to him.

"Sorry we've been so long," she whispered. "We couldn't get the ram and the wheelbarrow and us in all together. They're going back for it now."

Geoffrey slithered down to the water and found the wheelbarrow, which he hauled up to the road. By the time he'd brought the rest of the stores up the dinghy was back, with all three men in it.

"Thought I'd take her back, seeing as you were making the extra journey," whispered Mr Raison. "Don't want some busybody coming along and spotting her. Remember I can't get out if we have to leave after four a.m. I'll pooter off if you two aren't back by then,

Bas, and you'll have to lay low all day. Try and get down to that broken staging just below Buckler's Hard. I'll look for you there about eleven, and if you aren't there I'll try and come up here, but it won't be easy single-handed. Same the night after. Then I won't try any more, and you'll have to steal a boat, OK?"

"Aye, aye, sir," said the brothers together. As Mr Raison sculled away into the shadows they picked up the ungainly ram and carried it to the wheelbarrow. Geoffrey helped stack whatever stores they could round it, and the rest – mostly petrol – they hid in deep shadow under the old Abbey wall.

The main gate was locked, and though the key fitted the lock it wouldn't turn it. Arthur produced an oil can from a pocket and they tried again. Geoffrey was just feeling in the barrow for the big boltcutters when the corroded wards remembered their function. Arthur oiled the hinges, and after one ugly screech the gates swung silently open. Geoffrey shut them behind him.

The lock to the front door of the museum would not move at all, but the smaller door round on the far side gave easily enough, and they were in. The cars lay ghostly to left and right, lumpy blobs under their plastic foam and dust sheets. The floor was grey with dust, and

Geoffrey was surprised that he could see it, until he realised that the moon must now be up – he hadn't noticed in the tense crouching over the locks. He looked behind him, and saw in the dust four sets of footprints, like those black shoe-shapes which comic artists draw to show the reeling passage of a drunk along a pavement. One of the brothers lit a pencil torch, and in its stronger light Geoffrey could see little puffs of dust smoking out behind each heel as they put their feet down. Silence lay round them like a dream. Geoffrey had been against risking the tell-tale rubber wheel on the barrow – he'd felt they'd have been safer with good medieval iron muffled in canvas – but now he realised he'd been wrong. As they floated round the corner to where the Rolls ought to be the thud of his excited blood seemed the loudest noise in the night.

"That's her," said Basil.

"Aye," said Arthur. "That there lump on 'er bonnet's where the silver lady stands. Drape a bit of your bedding atween those two there, Jeff, and we won't hardly show no light."

Basil was already scratching with his fingernail at the white goo beneath the projection Arthur had pointed at. He tore a strip of the stuff away and shone his torch on the hole. They all saw the overlapping RR.

"Aye, that's her," said Arthur, and chuckled in the darkness. Geoffrey ran a cord between projections from the two white lumps on their right and draped sleeping bags into the gap. Arthur lit a small lantern torch and began tearing systematically at the cocooning plastic. Geoffrey untied the dustsheets that covered the rear two-thirds of the machine and found that the dash and the controls had also been cocooned. He helped Sally into the driver's seat and set her pecking sleepily away, then went off with the barrow to fetch the rest of the stores. By the time he'd finished his third trip, Basil and Arthur had torn off all the cocooning that would come easily, and were working under the bonnet, swabbing down the plastic with solvent. It shrivelled as the sponges touched it to a few small yellow blobs, which they wiped away with cloths. Sally was fast asleep on the front seat, sucking her thumb in a mess of white plastic. She grunted like a porker as Geoffrey heaved her into the back, but stayed there. He covered her with a blanket, swept out the litter of cocoon and started to swab away at the dash. She'd done pretty well, really. He finished the dash, cleared the steering wheel, gear lever and brake, and climbed down to see how the brothers were doing. They'd almost finished.

"I'll nip down and get that last jerry can," he said. "Then I'll give you a hand with the wheels and the ram."

"OK, Jeff. I reckon she'd start now – if she'll start at all."

Outside the moon was well up, leaving only the big stars sharp in a black sky. And something else was different. He stood still, and realised that the night was no longer noiseless. There was a muttering in the air. As he walked down to the gate he recognised it as the sound of low, excited voices. There was dim, flickering light beyond the bars – a lantern! He crept through the clotted mat of grasses, that had fallen during five summers of neglect into the drive, and peeped round the stone gatepost. There were three or four men on the grass bank where they'd landed on the other side of the road. The one with the lantern knelt and pointed. Another ran off to the sleeping houses. They must have spotted the tread-marks of the barrow's tyre. As quickly as he could move in silence, Geoffrey loped back to the museum. The brothers had hauled the ram in position in front of the bonnet and were standing scratching their heads.

"There's no time for that! They've spotted the barrow-tracks, or something. One of them ran off to the village!"

"Ah," said Basil, slowly, as though someone had told him crops were moderate this year.

"What'd we better do?" said Arthur, as though he already knew the answer but was just asking for politeness.

"Do you really think she'd start?"

"Ay. We've put some petrol in her, and primed her, and pumped her. Mebbe we could be getting off to some tidy spot in the Forest now, and put the old ram on there."

"What about the tyres?"

"Reckon we must go chancing that, Jeff. They don't look too bad to me. I'll be pumping her up while Basil puts the rest of the clobber in and you can see if she'll go. Oil's OK."

Geoffrey and Basil unfastened the absurd great straps which held the hood forward, eased the framework back and folded the canvas in. Sally said "I'm all right" as he lugged her back into the front seat to make room for the stores, but she stayed asleep. Then he settled himself behind the wheel, whispering to himself "Be calm. Be calm." Arthur was standing by the offside front wheel, methodically pawing away at the foot-pump, when Geoffrey moved the advance/retard lever up and switched on. Basil swung the starting handle, but nothing happened. The same the second time, but at the third swing the engine kicked, hiccuped and then all six cylinders woke to a booming purr. He revved a couple of times, and Arthur grinned at him through the easy note of power. This, thought Geoffrey, was far the most beautiful toy that man had ever made for himself. The idea was spoilt as a snag struck him. He gazed up the narrow and twisting path between the shrouded cars to the intractably locked main doors.

"How are we going to get out?" he shouted, though there was no need to shout. At low revs the engine made no more noise than a breeze in fir trees, but panic raised his voice.

"Ah," said Basil. He walked round and kicked the wall behind the car.

"This is nobbut weatherboarding here," he said. "I got a saw somewhere, and I'll be through that upright in a brace of shakes."

Arthur didn't even look up from his work. His long, pale face was flushed with the steady pumping, and there was a pearl or two of sweat on his moustache.

"All I ask is have a care the roof don't come down atop of us," he said.

Basil scratched his jaw and looked up at the crossbeam.

"Don't reckon she should," he said. "Not till we're out, leastways."

He took his saw from his toolbag and sawed with long, unhurried strokes at the upright timber. When he was through at the bottom he stood on two jerry cans and started again about seven foot from the ground. Arthur packed the pump into the back and went round the car, kicking the tyres thoughtfully. Basil jumped down from his pedestal and heaved the cans into the back. He looked over the door at the sleeping Sally, climbed up, picked her up gently and stowed her on the floor in front of the passenger seat. Then he lifted the sleeping bags off the cord and tucked them round and over her, until she was cushioned like an egg in an egg box. He knelt on the seat and reached over into the back, feeling in his toolbag, and brought out two hefty spanners. He handed one to Arthur and settled into the passenger seat.

"What's the spanner for?" asked Geoffrey.

"Bang folk with – if it comes to that. You see us out, Art. Follow us sharpish. I dunno how long that bit o' timber will stand. Reverse her out, Jeff, nice and steady. You got three tons o' metal there, pushing for you. Right?"

"Right," said Geoffrey, and moved the long lever through the gate into reverse. He let the handbrake off, revved gently and put the clutch in. There was about five foot to go, and Arthur, standing a little to one side, shone the torch on to the back wall. They were rolling backwards. With a foot to go Geoffrey put the accelerator down a full two inches, so that they would hit the wall slowly but with full power. He felt a dull jar, and at the same time the huge engine bunched its muscles and shoved. Timbers groaned and cracked. Splintered ends of wood screeched against the metal. The air was cold round his neck and shoulders, and he was no longer breathing dust and exhaust fumes. They were out.

He stopped, and Arthur walked out of the black cavern they had left, still holding the torch. The hut leaned a little sideways, but decided to stay up.

"Very nice," said Basil. "Reckon the drive's up thataway. You can push straight through that bit of old hedge. No, Art, don't you stay on the running board. They might clutch you off. I left a spot for you to squat on them cans, so you can look after that side, in case anyone tried to board us."

"What about the gates?" said Geoffrey.

"They'll give outwards, easy enough. I noticed that when we come in."

"OK," said Geoffrey.

He put the gears into first and drove forwards across the tangle of old lawn at the lonicera hedge. The ground was true and firm under the four-foot grasses, and the hedge gave easily. Then up to the drive, which seemed no wider than a bridle path now that they had the full width of the Rolls to occupy it. He turned towards the gates, outlined against several jigging lanterns, and changed (badly) into second. The villagers must have heard the crash.

But suddenly, behind the left-hand wall, stood up a great smoky flame, blazing into the night to a belling of whooping voices.

"Oy-oy," said Arthur, "they've found a spot of petrol. D'you leave a can there, Jeff?"

Before he could answer the tone of the voices changed; someone had heard the crash of gears, and now had seen the Rolls. The gates banged open and the drive was blocked by a barricade of people, black against the glare.

"Keep going," said Arthur, "fast as you can, remembering you got to get round the corner outside. Don't you pay no heed to *them*. They'll claw us limb from limb if you stop."

Geoffrey stayed in second, not risking a stall during another gear change, and put his foot down. The people leaped towards him, black and screaming. Arthur leaned forward and squeezed the bulb horn, which pooped its noble note. Basil stood up and bellowed "Out of the road there! Jump for it!" He couldn't help hitting someone now, but he kept accelerating, remembering the spearmen on Weymouth beach. The villagers, it turned out, were fewer than they looked and well inside the gates with room to scatter to safety. The car missed them all, somehow, and a volley of stones clunked into the bodywork as Geoffrey took her through the gate. He braked hard in the entrance, swung left, and revved again. There was a barrier of burning petrol across the road; a man in a priest's robes and holding a cross leaped for the running board and clung there, screaming Latin, until

Basil rapped him fiercely on the knuckles and he dropped off, howling, at the edge of the flame.

There were in it. Through it. In blackness. Geoffrey, blinded after the light, eased to a crawl for fear of going off the road. Arthur passed the torch forward and Basil adjusted its beam to shine twenty feet in front of them. It wasn't much, but it was enough. There were away.

A couple of miles on they stopped and listened for pursuit. Geoffrey kept the engine idling while the brothers fixed the main acetylene lamps. Then they drove on through the darkness, looking for a glade to hide in for the rest of the night. The road was awful.

5

NORTH

There was a breakfasty smell when Geoffrey woke, cramped and uneasy on the back seat. Arthur had built a small wood fire and was frying bacon.

"I wasn't certain as how I could get the Primus going," he said uneasily. "We'd better be starting on the old ram afore we can't tell one end of a spanner from t'other."

Sally was mooning around in the long grasses of the clearing, not looking at the Rolls. When they sat down on groundsheets for breakfast she made sure she had her back to it.

"Are you really going to be all right, Bas?" said Geoffrey.

"I reckon so. We go some oldish clobber on, and we *are* sailors. We can say we're going looking for work at Buckler's Hard. On'y thing is, do we *look* right? They don't all wear beards, do they, Sal?"

"No. It's just that they don't like shaving. It hurts. But the fussy ones go to the barbers to be shaved once a week."

The brothers sat around when they'd finished eating, as if they didn't want to start work. Geoffrey noticed Basil glancing sulkily at the car, and looking away again. In the end he had to say "Come on," and go and try to drag the ram round by himself. It was heavy and awkward, a pointed prow of cross-braced girders which kept poking sharp corners in under the mat of fallen grass and sticking. After he'd lugged it a few feet, Arthur came and helped. Between them they carried it round to the front of the Rolls, where Arthur tried to line it up back to front.

"Are you feeling all right, Arthur?" said Geoffrey.

"I dunno. I'm fine in myself, I suppose, but I don't feel certain of anything no more. Here, catch ahold of this, Bas, and help me hold it up for Jeff to buckle on. He can't do it hisself, not possibly."

Basil came across, muttering, and helped his brother lift the contraption and hold it in place while Geoffrey clamped it on to the dumb-irons in front of the car and then lay under the machine to fasten the long arms that ran back from it to the chassis. It took much longer than it should have, because the brothers were so awkward, Arthur giggling a little at his clumsiness, Basil sullen and ashamed. When he'd finished he went round to the front and looked at the result. Arthur came and stood beside him, hands on hips.

"Do you think it will really do the trick, Arthur?"

"Should do. Leastways we worked it out pretty careful in France. But I wouldn't be knowing now. Not beautiful, is she?"

Geoffrey wasn't sure whether he was referring to the ram alone, or (now that the effect of England was clearly beginning to work on him), to the car itself. The ram was certainly ugly, crude in its red-lead paint, brutal, jutting out three foot in front of the proud radiator like a deadly cowcatcher. They'd feel pretty silly if they turned out not to need it after all, Geoffrey thought, as he primed the cylinders and pumped pressure into the tank.

"D'you feel like helping me with the tyres?" he said.

"Not really, to speak honest, Jeff. You can manage 'em by yourself, surely."

"I expect so. I'll have to take her out on to the road so that the jack doesn't sink, and perhaps you and Basil could keep a lookout for me... What is it, Sal?"

She came running from the end of the glade.

"There's something enormous in the woods, Jeff. I can hear it crashing about. Do you think it's a dragon?"

Geoffrey laughed. "Most likely a pony," he said. But neither Arthur nor Basil looked amused.

"Best get everyone into the car," said Arthur. "Think you can start her by yourself, Jeff?"

They could all hear the crashing now. It sounded like a tank blundering about in the undergrowth. Then the noise changed, as the thing began to charge straight towards them, ignoring thicket and brake. Geoffrey swung the engine and ran round to the driver's seat. They all waited, looking sideways towards the noise, where the mid-morning sunlight stood in shafts of warmth against the darkness under the oaks. A bush convulsed and opened, and in a patch of light stood a prodigious boar, tusked, hairy, slavering, not twenty yards away. It shook itself and swung its low-held head from side to side, inspecting the glade. Its tiny red eye seemed to blaze as it spotted the car, and it grunted as though that was what it had come for. At once it was careering towards them, a wild, fierce missile of hard muscle and harder bone. Geoffrey let the clutch in with a bang. The wheels spun on the grass, then gripped, and they were moving, accelerating, out over the layers of leaves the brothers had spread to camouflage their tracks, into second, third, doing fifty over the potholes, away.

Three hundred yards down the tarmac he eased up and craned over his shoulder. The boar was sitting on its haunches in the middle of the arch under the trees, watching them go. It still looked enormous eighty yards back.

"They don't come that big," said Basil in a low voice. "'Tisn't natural."

"I don't know," said Geoffrey. "You get farm pigs as big as that, with proper breeding. I wouldn't be surprised if a lot of farm pigs have escaped and gone wild since the Changes. How close did it get?"

"Six foot or so," said Arthur. "Dunno that it would have done any real harm, unless it had nicked a tyre. Hope there's not many of them about, eh, Bas?"

"Looked like it was coming for the car, not for us," said Basil.

They both sounded sick and bewildered, quite

different from the calm and assured couple who had helped him steal the Rolls. Geoffrey realised that he had them on his hands now, and that he ought to make it as easy as possible for them to get back to the river by nightfall.

"Let's have a squint at that map," he said. "Look here. I think the best thing would be if I took you on up to Lyndhurst and then turned south. I've got to go there – there doesn't seem to be any real way round it. Then I can run you down almost to Brockenhurst and you can take the B3055 back to Beaulieu – it looks about six miles, and you don't want to come back along the road we left by. You needn't go into the village at all, actually, which is a good thing because it's probably still humming. I can go off this side road here, almost to Lyndhurst, and then right up this one here, which'll bring me back on to the road I was going to take anyway, up through the Wallops. Cheer up, Bas. I daresay you'll feel better once you're away from the Rolls."

"Hope so."

Lyndhurst was a ghost town, almost. There were no money-bringing tourists now, and the Forest, wilder than before, did not provide enough income to support

83

a community. They boomed down deserted streets, left and left again. An old man leaning on a staff watching sheep graze a stretch of close-nibbled common turned at the sound of the motor, shook his fist at them and shouted something indistinguishable. But a curse, for certain.

When he judged he was just out of earshot of Brockenhurst Geoffrey stopped. The brothers climbed out and stood dully in the road.

"Now listen," Geoffrey said. "You go down here for about half a mile and turn left. Got that? It's just where the stream crosses the road. You'd better take your bag, Basil, but leave out anything modern. Here; I'll sort it out for you. Saw, hammer, chisels, cold chisel, these square nails should be OK, hand drill, bits, brace, no, not the hacksaw, I should think – that'll have to do. Here are four gold pieces in case you have to lie up for a bit, and need to buy food."

"They'll have to think of a story for them," said Sally. "They're a lot of money, and people always ask."

"All right. Now listen. You've been working in a shipyard at Bristol as carpenter and mate, and the master died and you didn't like the new master. So you thought you'd try your luck down this way. Got that?"

Basil glanced sideways at Arthur, doubtfully, but Arthur nodded. Geoffrey realised that he'd been speaking loud and slow, as if to a stupid kid. He went on at the same pace.

"Don't go into Beaulieu if you can help it. Wait for two nights at the disused piles below the Hard. If you don't meet Mr Raison, steal a boat and sail south. Take food with you, and don't try to do it in a rowing boat. It's too far. It's a hundred miles. Got it? OK, off you go. Goodbye, and thank you very much for all you've done. I'll wait till you're clear, off our road, so that people aren't watching for anything special when you pass. Good luck."

Basil spoke, slowly and thickly.

"I wonder if we done right, after all."

He was looking with loathing at the Rolls.

Geoffrey caught Arthur's eye and jerked his head sideways.

"Come along now, Bas," said Arthur. "We best be stepping along. Bye, Jeff and Sally, and good luck to you, I suppose."

The brothers turned together and walked off down the road, their shapes black in the stretches of sunlight and almost invisible in the shadows of the trees. At first they trudged listlessly, like tired men (which indeed they must have been), but after a while their backs straightened, their heads moved as if they had begun to talk to each other, and their pace became springier. At the curve of the road, beyond which they would no longer be seen, they stopped in the sunlight, turned and waved – a real goodbye this time, friendly and encouraging even at this distance. Then they were out of sight.

"I hope they'll be all right," said Geoffrey. "I was dead worried when they went all fuzzy like that, but they seemed to perk up once they were a bit away from the car. We'd never have got here without them. Does this thing worry *you*, Sal?"

"Some of the time. But I don't think it really bothers me *inside* me, if you see what I mean. Not like Arthur and Basil. It was something in their minds coming out which made them go all funny. But with me it's really only that I'm not used to engines. I'm used to thinking they're wicked. Parson preached against machines every Sunday, almost. He said they were the abomination of deserts and the great beast in the Bible. He watched the men stoning Uncle Jacob."

"But you aren't suddenly going to drop a match into our petrol tank?"

"I don't expect so. I don't feel any different from France. I hated those little French beetles whining about, but I think some machines are lovely, like the train on the bridge. And this one too, I suppose."

She ran a dirty hand over the old red leather.

"Then you must be immune, too, or you'd have started going like the brothers. Do you think it runs in families? There was Uncle Jacob, and you, and me. Do you really think we're the only ones?"

"I don't know. I don't *feel* like an only one."

"Nor do I. I think I must have been immune before I got hit on the head, or I'd never have been able to look after *Quern*. I suppose Uncle Jacob told me—"

"Jeff, I think there's another animal coming. I can feel it."

"OK, Sal."

He let the big engine take the car slowly away, trying not to disturb the murderous forest which had sent the boar, but it was too late. A grey stallion, wild, swerved into the road ahead of them, snorted as it saw the car and reared with whirling hooves to meet them. Geoffrey increased his speed, nudged the wheel over so that the ram pointed directly at the beast and pooped the horn. The stallion squealed back. At the last moment, when they were doing nearly forty, he jerked the wheel to the left and back again, so that the huge car skittered sideways and on. The horse, clumsy on its hind legs, couldn't turn in time to block them, but a hoof, unshod, banged on metal somewhere at the back of the car.

They drove quietly round the outskirts of Brockenhurst until they came on a group of children playing a complicated sort of hopscotch in the middle of the road. The girls ran screaming into the houses, but the boys picked up clods and stones out of the gutter and showered them at the Rolls, which clanged like a tinsmith's shop as Geoffrey nosed through. The windscreen starred on Sally's side, where a flint caught it. A man came and stood in a doorway with a steaming mug in his hand. He shouted and flung it at the car, but missed completely in his rage and the mug shattered against the wall of a cottage on the far side, leaving great splodges like blood on the white stucco.

Geoffrey laughed as he accelerated away. "Tomato soup," he said.

Sally was crying. "It's everybody hating us, even the children. It's horrid."

"They hated the car, really. They'd have been sure to '

hit one of us if they'd really been aiming at us. Cheer up, Sal. We're not going through any more towns. We've chosen a whole lot of little lanes that ought to miss them completely, and you'll have to do the map reading. I'll teach you as soon as we come to a safe bit of straight where we can't get surprised."

They found a good place almost at once, by a stream under some willows. Geoffrey stopped the car and switched off the engine.

"It's quite easy," he said, "especially as we're going north so everything's the right way round. These yellow and green and red lines are the roads. That's all that matters for the moment, but you'll learn the other signs as we go along. That's Brockenhurst, which we've just been through, and we're here. We want to get up to this road with the pencil mark beside it, which is the one we're supposed to be on, so we go up here, see, to the A35. That's about three miles. Then we turn right, and quite soon come to a bridge – this blue line is the river. Then a bit over a mile further on, when we're almost in Lyndhurst, we turn left through Emery Down and we're on our proper road. Try and tell me what's going to happen next about a mile before we get to it. Right? Off we go."

What happened next was a tree across the road. It had evidently been there a couple of years, but nobody had tried to move it. Instead, passers-by had beaten a rutted track round the bole, which Geoffrey had to follow. The Rolls lurched and heaved at a walking pace, with the ruts, hardened by months of summer, wrenching the steering wheel about. Geoffrey remembered what the military-looking gentleman had told him about Silver Ghosts being used in the First World War to carry despatches through the shell-raddled terrain behind the trenches. He realised, too, that he still had the five-year-old tyres on. The ram was a nuisance in the tight curve of the track, poking ahead and catching in brambles and old man's beard, but the big engine wrenched it through. It might come in useful soon: the A35 was the old main road between Southampton and Bournemouth, and there was that bridge. He swung back thankfully on to the remains of the old tarmac.

A couple of miles later he eased cautiously out on to the main road. Its surface was no better than that of the sidelanes – worse, if anything, as it seemed to have seen more traffic – but it was wide enough for him to pick some sort of path between the potholes. They swirled past a cart, leaving the driver to shout the usual curse through their long wake of dust. Now that they were coming out of the forest, there would be more people about, of course. The road dipped towards the stream, and there was the bridge.

And there, on the bridge, was the tollgate. Sally had mentioned tollgates to M. Pallieu, who had informed the General. The ram had been built on his instructions. It was his sort of weapon.

The gate looked hideously solid, with a four-inch beam top and bottom, set into a huge post at either side. Geoffrey changed down to third and second, double de-clutching anxiously. The tollkeeper, a fat woman in a white apron, came to the door of her cottage, stared up the road and screeched over her shoulder. Geoffrey changed down (beautifully – the military-looking gentleman would have been delighted) into first, glanced at the gate – now only twenty foot away – decided he was still going too fast and eased off, to a trot, to a walk. With the gate a yard off he accelerated. The whole car jarred through all its bones as the ram slammed into the bottom beam – they weren't going to make it. With a deep twang the hinges gave, the structure lifted and leapt sideways, and the car surged forwards. A big man with an orange beard pushed out from behind the woman, swinging a sledgehammer, but before he got within smiting distance a yellow thing looped out of the car behind Geoffrey's head and caught him in the face. Unbalanced by the swing of his hammer he fell backwards, bringing the fat woman down too. Geoffrey drove on.

"What on earth was that that hit him?" he asked.

"I threw your smelly stove at him," said Sally. "I never liked it anyway. I hope they aren't all as exciting as that."

"With luck we won't meet many. We'll hardly be on main roads at all. But rivers are almost the only thing we can't find a way round, so we've got to go over bridges. I didn't expect the gates to be quite so strong as that."

"We turn left quite soon," said Sally. "When are we going to have lunch?"

"Let's drive on a bit. I don't really want to stop till I need a rest from driving. There ought to be some biscuits somewhere. If we get a puncture we'll just have to stop."

6

ROUGH PASSAGE

They found an open lift of chalk an hour later, between Winchester and Salisbury, roughly, where an old chalkpit opened off the road. Geoffrey drove in between the high banks and discovered that the place had been used, in civilised days, as a graveyard for abandoned cars. There were a dozen rusting saloons amid the nettles and elders.

The floor of the pit was hard enough to hold a jack. Sally climbed up with the food to the untended grassland above the pit and kept a lookout while he changed the tyres. (These came already attached to their steel rims, which were then bolted to the wooden wheels – it couldn't have been easier.) That left him with two good spares and the four old ones. He climbed up and joined Sally.

The Rolls was invisible from a few yards, but they could see for leagues. The countryside to the south, which had once been mile-square fields, had reverted to a mosaic of tiny, unrelated patches, some worked, some abandoned. After half a mile away to the south he could see a piece of green with a row of dots spread across it at the line where the green changed texture. He ate a slab of bread and camembert and saw that the dots had moved – they were a team of men mowing a hayfield with scythes. Behind them came another pattern of dots, again altering the texture of the green: more men (or probably women) tossing the hay out of its scythe-laid rows so that every stem and blade was exposed to the reliable sun. A few fields away they'd got beyond that stage and were loading the pale, dried hay on to a wooden wagon. Elsewhere the cereal crops were still tender green, oat and wheat and barley each showing its different shade in long narrow strips. The sun was very hot, and there were lots of butterflies, all the species regenerated since men stopped spraying. Geoffrey felt tired as tired.

"I think I'd better try and have a nap, Sal, or I might drive off the road. Wake me up the moment you see anything funny. You'd better put everything back in the car, so that if we really are caught napping we can say we had nothing to do with it. We just found it, and were waiting for someone to come along and tell us what to do next. I'll stick to my robe, just in case. Remember, I'm your idiot brother, deaf and dumb but quite harmless, and you're in charge of me, trying to get us north to stay with our married sister in, um, Staffordshire. You take the grub down, and I'll see if I can find a place without too many ants."

"When do you want to wake up, supposing nothing happens?"

"Give me a couple of hours, about."

He rolled up his jersey with the robe inside it for a pillow, and wriggled round for a place where his hip felt comfortable. The grass ticked with insect life. The sun was very bright. A seedhead tickled his cheek. Hell, he wasn't going to be able to sleep here....

"Wake up, Jeff. Wake up."

He sat up, the side of his face nubbly with knit-work of the jersey. The sun had moved, and the mowers were near the end of their field. The wagon was gone, and the air was still and heavy with grass-pollen.

"I'm sorry, Jeff. You've slept for about three hours, but they've pulled that haywain on to this road, and I think they'll be bringing it up the hill. They're going awfully slowly. There. You can see them coming out by that copse."

A green-gold hump heaved into sight out of the trees. There was a man in blue overalls lying on his back on top of it, with his hand behind his head. The wagon was about the size of a Dinky toy, and it would be ages before the horses brought it creaking up the hill.

"Anything happen while I was asleep?"

"Nothing, except that a rabbit came and nibbled one of the wheels, but I threw stones at it and it ran away."

Geoffrey lunged down the slope to look at his tyres. On the off front there was a series of strong gouges, running in pairs – not nibbling, but a determined attack. The wain was still a good twenty minutes off, he decided – not worth risking a tyre like that over these roads. He got the jack out, fumbled it into position, pulled himself together and changed the wheel deliberately. Eight minutes, not bad. There was time to fill up with petrol. Its stench rose shimmering into the untainted air. Four gallons gone.

As they backed out on to the road there were shouts from down the hill. Three men with hayforks, very red in the face, were running slowly up towards them. Golly, they must have spotted the tyre treads in a patch of chalk dust on the untended tarmac. Lucky he'd been given as much as three hours' sleep – the countryside must be fantastically empty for nobody to have come up the road in all that time. The Rolls whined to the top in second and hummed down the far side, leaving the haymakers shouting. One of them had been wearing a smock, of the kind you used to see in particularly soppy nursery-rhyme books.

On the next long stretch of road he stopped and sorted out the most obviously French blanket. This he folded in two, with the tent pole on the fold; he ran about six foot of cord from each corner of the hood at the back of the car to the two projecting ends of pole; then he made a couple of holes through the blankets and tied the pole in.

"What's that for?" said Sally.

"Sweep out our tracks, with luck."

"It won't last very long, I'd have thought. Haven't

97

you got anything tougher, like a piece of canvas or something?"

"No."

"What about cutting some branches out of the hedge. You could tie them in two bunches, and it wouldn't matter if they wore a bit, because there'd always be more twigs coming down."

"I suppose that'd work, too, but let's see how we get on with this first."

They drove on. Sally kneeling in her seat and looking backwards. The blanket lasted about three miles. Sally hummed perkily as she helped him cut two large besoms of brushwood and tie them where the blanket had been. Off they went again. Sally still watching backwards.

"It's making a terrible lot of dust, Jeff – much more than before."

Hell. He ought to have thought of that, with the roads so white with powder from the chalk hills. They were sending up a signal for miles in every direction. Better to leave tracks behind than warn people you were coming. He stopped, climbed down again and cut the bundles free.

Just outside Over Wallop they came round a corner

to find a high-piled haywain clean across the road, manoeuvring to back into a farmyard. Geoffrey braked hard. There was no hope of turning in the narrow lane before the farm workers were on them – he'd have to reverse out and find a way round. But before he came to a complete stop the carthorses panicked, rearing and squealing as they struggled to escape through the quickset hedge opposite the farm gate. The wain came with them, up to its shafts, leaving a possible gap behind it. He wrenched the gear into first and banged through, misjudging it slightly so that the near mudguards grated against the farm wall. Amid the grinding and shouting he was aware of a portentous figure poised in midair above him, arms raised, spear brandished, like St Michael treading down the dragon. He ducked as the man on top of the hay flung his missile, but the hayfork clanged into the bonnet and stuck there, flailing from side to side, as he drove on into the village. He couldn't afford to stop and pull it out until he was well clear of the houses, by which time it had wrenched two hideous wounds in the polished aluminium. Thank heavens Lord Montagu wasn't there to see how his toy was being treated.

The railway bridge over the road at Grately was

down, and they had to grind up the embankment, jolt over the deserted rails and lurch down the far side, the ram twanging the rusty fence-wire as if it had been thread.

Three quarters of an hour later they were driving towards Inkpen Beacon, just south of Hungerford. The westering sun lay broad across the land, and under the bronze, horizontal light the hollows and combes were already filling with dusk. Above the purr of the engine and the hiss of the passing air they heard a hallooing on the hill above them; the gold horizon was fringed with horsemen, who were careering along the ridge of down to cut across their path where the road climbed to the saddle. Geoffrey grinned to himself. There was still a couple of hundred yards of flat to allow him to take a run at the incline, so there was no need to change down. He pressed firmly on the accelerator and the sighing purr rose to a solid boom; the feel of the wheel hardened in his hands and the rose-tangled hedges blurred with backward speed. The military-looking gentleman had told him that a single-seater Silver Ghost, stripped for racing, had done a hundred miles an hour at Brooklands; this one was supposed to do seventy in its whining sprint gear, but he wasn't using that on a hill – third should do it. The needle stood just over fifty as the bonnet tilted to take the meat of the twisting slope. Sally laughed beside him.

The horsemen were hidden now, behind the false crest of the down, and the engine, losing the impetus of its first rush, changed its note to a creamy gargle and swung them up the hill at a workaday forty. The hedges gave way to open down as the Rolls swept towards the top and there were the horsemen again, coming along the ridge track at a whooping gallop, a dozen of them, barely fifty yards away. They hadn't a hope, except for the little man who led them on the big roan with a hawk on his wrist and his green cloak swirling behind him. He was barely six yards off when the Rolls, bucketing in a bad patch of pothole, hurtled over the saddle and whisked away down into the sudden cutting on the northern slope. Sally twisted in her seat to watch the hunters.

"That was fun," she said.

"Yes. What did they do?"

"They talked and waved their arms and then one of them started to gallop off that way. Wait a sec while I look at the map. I think he was going to Hungerford."

"Bother. That front chap looked like someone

important, and he'll get them to send messengers out to warn the countryside. That means it won't be safe to stop for at least another twenty miles, and I'd been hoping to camp for the night before long. I'd better fill up with petrol now, to be on the safe side. D'you think there'll be another tollgate at – where is it?"

"Kintbury."

There was – a re-used level-crossing gate, with its oil lanterns still on it. They left it in spillikins, crossed the A4 and boomed up the hill to Wickham, where they swung left on to the old Roman road to Cirencester, Ermine Street. It was busier than any road they'd been on. Haymakers were coming home now, through the dusty brown shadows of evening; old crones led single cows back to the byres; courting couples walked entwined through the shadier passages beneath arched beeches; the odd rider spurred towards some engagement. Twice Geoffrey had to swing on to the verge and jolt round a towering wagon with its team of fear-crazed horses (small horses – five years is nothing like long enough to revive the strain of the huge, strong, patient Shires, which hauled for our ancestors for generations before the tractor came). The second time Sally was hit on the arm by the blunt side of a flung sickle, just at the moment when Geoffrey felt his offside front wheel slithering into a hidden ditch beneath the grass. Raging, he wrenched at the live wheel and stamped on the accelerator. It happened to be the right thing to do, and the car roared free, nudging the corner of the wagon so that the whole cargo, already unsettled by the antics of the horses, tilted sideways and settled on the man who had thrown the sickle.

"It's not bad," said Sally, "honestly. It's just a sort of thin bruise. Crimminy though, this thing's sharp on the other side."

At Baydon there was some sort of merrymaking or religious procession or something in the main street (which is all Baydon consists of). Anyway it involved a lot of hand-drawn carts with a ring of candles round the rim of each, very pretty in the dusk-tinged night. The villagers were all in fancy dress, looking like dolls on a souvenir stall, but jumped squawking for safety as Geoffrey, still stupid with rage at a society where grown men felt it was proper to throw deadly tools at his kid sister, clove into the procession. The ram splintered the handcarts. Candles cartwheeled into the shadows. Women shrilled and men bellowed. On the other side of the village they were in blackness, real night, with a lot of stars showing.

"Time to find somewhere to sleep, Sal. See if you can spot a place which looks empty on the map. I don't mind turning off this road if we have to."

"Anywhere for the next six or seven miles, I think." (Sally had Arthur's pencil torch out.) "After that we come to a sort of plain which seems absolutely crammed with villages, and then we've got to turn off and start wiggling, which I'd rather not do in the dark."

They found a spot, a couple of miles on, where the road dipped over the shoulder of a hill and eased to the right to take the gentler slope. But a still earlier age had preferred to cut the corner, and it was possible to drive down the old track – as old, perhaps, as the Romans – into a natural lay-by. They were only fifteen yards from the road, but hidden by a thorn thicket. Geoffrey left the engine running and scouted off into the dark to make sure he could get out at the far end, if need be. Then, while Sally rummaged for a cold supper and the engine clicked as it cooled, he unrolled a ball of twine and rigged a kind of tripwire all round the car. They sat, backs to the warm radiator, in the balmy dark and ate garlic sausage, processed cheese, bread and tomatoes, and drank the last of the Coca-Cola.

"You aren't frightened of *this* car, Sal?"

"No. Not any longer. Really it's more like an animal – a super charger for rescuing princesses with. We've been frightfully lucky so far, haven't we, Jeff?"

"I suppose so. That was a nasty bit when we found the wagon across the road, and I suppose the other man could have hit you with the sharp side of his sickle." (He'd found it on the floor of the car, and it really had been sharp, honed like a carving knife.) "And other places too, honestly. I was scaredest at that first toll bridge, because it was something we'd planned for and didn't seem to be working. But we've *got* to be lucky, Sal, so there's no point in thinking about it."

"You're all like that. Boys and men, I mean. If there's no point in thinking about something, you don't. Are we going to sleep on the grass or in the car?"

"In the car. We aren't really far enough from Baydon for comfort. I'll prime the cylinders and put a bit of pressure in the tank, just in case we have to be off in a hurry. I wonder whether it's worth making a hill fog. It wouldn't be difficult tonight."

"Funny how you know about that when you can't remember anything else."

"I don't have to *remember* it. I just know."

"Anyway, don't let's have a fog. It would be a pity to spoil the stars."

It would too. It was a night when it was easy to believe in astrology. He tucked Sally into the back seat, filled the tank with petrol, put a quart of oil into the engine, looked into the radiator and realised they ought to stop for water at the first stream they came to, primed the cylinders, pumped the tank, tied the loose end of his trip-string round his thumb and attempted to find a comfortable position across the front seats. He tried several attitudes, but really he was too long for the width of the car – it was as if a grown man was lying down in a child's cot. In the end he lay on his back, knees up, and started to count the ecstatic stars.

He was woken by Sally pinching his ear. It was still dark.

"Don't do that. Go back to sleep at once. Did you have a bad dream?"

"Sh. Listen."

League upon league the fields and woods lay round them, silent in an enchantment of dark. No, not quite silent. Somewhere to the south there was a faint but continuous noise, a rising and falling hoot, or howl, very eerie.

"What's that?"

"Hounds. Hunting. I've heard them before."

His mind flickered for an instant to the dog that had bayed on the banks of Beaulieu estuary, but whose cry had gone unanswered.

"What on earth are they hunting at this time of night?"

"Us."

Yes, possibly. The village of Baydon might have come swarming after them, like a hive of pestered bees. More likely the man with the hawk had sent a messenger to Hungerford and got a thorough pursuit organised. If he was important enough he could have commandeered fresh horses, fresh hounds even, all the way up. It wasn't all that distance.

"How far away are they? What time is it?"

Sally looked at the stars for a moment.

"Between three and four. I don't think they're as far off as they sound."

She was right. The hound cry modulated to a recognisable baying, only just up the road, a noise whose hysterical yelping note told that the dogs had scented their presence and not just their trail. The best bet was to start on the magneto: he switched on and flicked the advance and retard lever up and down. Too fast. He took it more slowly and the engine hummed alive. As he moved off there was a sudden biting pain in his right thumb. The damn string. He declutched and tugged. No go. He leant over and tried to bite the taut cord free, but achieved nothing more than saliva-covered string, as strong as ever. Suddenly the cord gave and something bonked into the bodywork beside his head – Sally had slashed the cord through with the sickle. The hounds sounded as if they were almost on them as Geoffrey eased the car over the loose rubble of the old road, jerked up on to the newer tarmac and accelerated downhill. The white dust of the road (limestone here) made the way easy to see under a large moon. They whined down the incline and curved into a long straight, overhung with beeches on the left and with a bare, brute hill shouldering out the stars on the other side. The surface was almost unpocked, and Geoffrey did fifty for six miles on end.

"Jeff! Jeff! You must slow down. I can't read the map in the dark at this speed. We've got to turn off somewhere along here and there's a stream just before. It may be another gate. No, it wasn't – that must have been it. Now we turn right in half a mile and then left almost at once, and then – oh, I see, you've only done that to get round Stratton St Margaret. It's awfully wiggly. Couldn't we go straight through at this time of night?"

They did, the exhaust calling throatily off the brick walls down the long street. Half the roofs showed starlight through them.

"Right here! Right!"

He only just got the car round on to the A361.

"I thought you said straight through."

"Well, it's straighter than going round, anyway. I'm sorry. We turn left in about three miles. I think I'll be able to see soon without the torch. Bother. We could have gone straight through and branched off later. It would have saved us a lot of wiggling."

"Never mind. If that's the main road to Cirencester there's probably quite a bit of stuff on it in the early hours – folk going to market and so on. I hope it gets lighter soon."

It did. The grey bars in the east infected the whole sky. The stars sickened. For about five minutes, while his eyes were adjusting to their proper function, he drove through a kind of mist which was really inside his own mind, because he couldn't decide how far down the road he could really see. Then it was morning, smelling of green grass sappy with dew. They breakfasted early, before the dew could clear and the haymakers would be about with their forks and scythes. Geoffrey filled the radiator from a cattle trough, still a bit shaken by the distance the hunt had managed to cover (assuming that it came from Hungerford – and he was sure it did – he was obsessed by the small man on the big horse with a hawk on his wrist) in seven hours or so. He got out the map and did sums. They'd done about twenty miles between Inkpen Beacon and stopping for the night, and roughly the same again this morning. At that rate the hunt, if it kept going, would be about twelve miles behind now. Allow an hour for breakfast, and it would be six miles – say four for safety. That should be OK.

But they must have spotted the general direction the Rolls was going by now, and they might send messengers posting up the main road to Cirencester and Cheltenham. If they took it seriously enough (and, considering Weymouth Bay and the fuss since the Rolls had been stolen and everything, there was no reason why they shouldn't) they might send more messengers along the main roads radiating from those towns, ordering a watch to be kept. Obviously all the bridges west of Gloucester would be closely guarded. The first danger point would be crossing the Fosse Way, a few miles on; then the A40 and A436. Besides, once people were about to mark their passage, there'd be messages and rumours streaming into the towns from the farmland, and the hunt would know which way its quarry had passed. Better not allow an hour for breakfast, really. They might be able to have a bit of a rest when they were up beyond Winchcombe and had turned sharply left.

Perhaps it was just luck, or perhaps it was because they'd kept going and left the chase miles behind, but they had almost no trouble all morning except for shaken fists and thrown stones. They motored in flawless summer between the walled fields of the Cotswolds, dipping into steep valleys where loud streams drove booming waterwheels, or where gold-grey wool towns throve in the sudden prosperity which the defeat of the machine had brought back from the north. Then up, hairpinning through hangers of beeches, where herds of pigs grunted after mast, watched by small boys in smocks. Or along moulded uplands where huge flocks of sheep nibbled at fields still rich from the forced harvests of six years back.

The only real excitement came from such a flock, which they met not far from Sudeley Castle in a bare lane with well-kept walls rising five feet on either side. The road foamed with fleeces for hundreds of yards, and beyond they could see a group of blue-clad drovers beginning to gesticulate at the sight of the car. There was time to hesitate. Geoffrey thought for a moment of ploughing on through a carnage of mutton, but realised he'd bog down almost at once.

"How far have I got to go round if we go back, Sal?"

"Miles."

"Oh well, let's see what happens."

He pulled over as far to the left as he could, and then swung right. This wasn't going to be like a gate. He slowed below a walking speed before the ram touched the wall. The whole car groaned, jarred and stopped, wheels spinning. He backed and charged the same spot, and this time saw the top of the wall waver. Third time it gave, and the Rolls heaved itself through the gap, one wheel at a time because of the angle, like a cow getting over a fence. The grass on the other side was almost as smooth as a football field, and they fetched a wide circuit round the flock. A flotilla of sheepdogs hurled across the green and escorted them, yelping, to a flimsy gate which the ram smashed through without trouble. Soon after he had settled to the road again he realised that the car did not feel itself.

"Lean out and look at the wheels, Sal."

"There's something wrong with this one on my side at the back. It's all squidgy."

He could see nothing through the wake of dust, but when he stopped and listened there seemed to be no sound of pursuit. He climbed down, leaving the engine running, and looked at the rear nearside wheel. The tyre was flat, with a big flap of rubber hanging away from the battered rim. When he was halfway through changing it there was a snarling scurry in the road and a black sheepdog sprang towards him, teeth bared. He lashed at it with the wrench, and it backed off and came again. He lashed again, and again it retreated. As it darted in for the third time a stone caught it square on the side of the jaw and it flounced, whining, out of range.

"I think I can keep it off for a bit, Jeff."

"Super. Golly, you're a good shot, Sal. Where did you learn that?"

"Scaring rooks."

When he had two nuts on she spoke again.

"There's someone coming down the road, and I think I saw a man running behind the wall over there. Something blue went past the gate at the other side of the field."

He hurriedly screwed on a third nut, hoping that that would be enough to hold for a few miles, and lowered the clumsy jack. As he drove off half a dozen men appeared from behind walls to left and right, like players at the end of a game of hide and seek. Heaven knows what kind of an ambush they'd been planning, given five minutes more. He stopped and put the remaining nuts on just before they turned left on the A438. They banged through another tollgate, over the Avon and climbed the embankment on to the M5 motorway near a place called Ripple. The great highway was a wound of barren cement through the green, lush pastures. It was deserted. Where they joined it there was a strange area, a black, charred circle covering both carriageways. Two miles later they came to another.

7

THE STORM

"Funny," said Geoffrey. "It looks as if someone had been lighting a series of enormous bonfires down here. D'you think they've been trying to burn the motorway?"

"It isn't quite like bonfires – it's too clean. There's always bits and bobs of ends of stick left round a bonfire, and the ash doesn't blow away either, not all of it. It makes itself into a sticky grey lump. It *is* funny. I suppose they *could* have come and swept it up."

There was something else funny too. Geoffrey felt it in a nook of his mind as being wrong, out of key with the solid sunshine of the day. There was a flaw in the weather ahead of them, a knot in the smooth grain of the sky. Nothing to see, unless it lay hidden beyond the hills of the Welsh border. It worried him, so much so that he kept glancing at the horizon and almost drove headlong into a vast pit in the road where a bridge had once carried the motorway but was now a scrawl of rusted and blackened iron. He let the weight of the car take them down the embankment and stopped in the lower road to look at the wreckage.

"It must have been a bomb did that, Sal."

"They don't have bombs. It's been burnt, hasn't it?"

Very odd. The destruction didn't look as if it had been done by people at all. He felt thoroughly uneasy as he drove up the far embankment. The flaw in the weather was insistent now, either stronger or closer – he thought he could see a change in the hue of the air just north of one of the hills on the western horizon. Another three miles and he was sure. Soon the shape of the hammerheaded cloud that brings thunder was unmistakable. Odd to see one of them, all alone, but nice to know what it was that had been worrying him. He drove on, relieved.

But soon his relief was replaced by a greater unease. Thunderclouds didn't move like that – they planed slowly across the countryside in straight lines, diffusing energy, grumbling, like an advance of arthritic colonels. This one was compact, purposeful, sweeping eastward down a single corridor of wind between the still regions of summer air. He increased his speed to get out of its path, the Rolls exulting up to seventy. At this speed they'd be clear of the cloud's track in no time.

Or would they? He slacked off and gazed at the hills again. The corridor must be curved, for the cloud was still advancing towards them, moving at a pace of a gale. A few miles more and there was no doubt about it – the thing was aimed at the Rolls, following as a homing missile follows its target. He stopped the car.

"Out you get, Sal, and up the bank. Two can play at that game."

He followed her slowly through the clinging weeds, gathering his strength, resting his mind. The motorway ran here through a deep cutting, from whose top he could see for some distance. He unrolled his jersey, took out the robe and put it on. Then he sat beside Sally and stared at the charging cloud, blue-black beneath and white with reflected sunshine through its two miles of height. The thing to do was nudge it aside. Wind from the south-west.

The island drowses with heat. The hills are baked. The mown hayfields drink sun. The woods breathe warmth. And over them all lies air, air twice heated, first as the jostling sunbeams plunge down, again as the purring earth gives back the warmth it cannot drink. Isle-wide the air swells with sunlight, lightening as it swells, rising as it lightens, sucking in more air beneath it, cold from the kiss of the Atlantic. Now it comes, broad-fronted over the Marches, comes now,

   here,

      now,

         here,

            now in this darkness, in this up and down roaring of black, rubbing itself together, three miles high, generating giant forces, poised, ready, smiting down with a million million volts on to the thing it was aimed at...

Mastered, overwhelmed, Geoffrey crumpled into a gold shambles. Sally alone, thumbs uselessly in her ears, watched the storm heave its bolts of bellowing light down on the Rolls. The air stank with ozone. The clay of the bank vibrated like a bass string. She rolled on to her belly, buried her face in the grasses and screamed.

The noise was gone, except inside her skull. Dully

she sat up and looked down the embankment at the motorway. The Rolls, charred and twisted, lay in the centre of a circle of blackened cement like the others she had seen. Tyres and upholstery smoked, the stench of burnt rubber, leather and horsehair reeking up the bank on the remains of Geoffrey's wind. The wind had carried the cloud away, appeased. Her brother lay beside her on his back, with bruise-blue lips and cheeks the colour of whitewash. She thought he was dead until she slid her hand under the robe and felt the movement of his breathing.

When a person faints you keep him warm and give him sweet tea. She must get his jersey on, but not over the robe in case someone came by. It was like trying to dress a huge lead doll, and took ages. But it was three hours more before he woke.

Geoffrey came to to the sound of voices. There seemed to be several people about. He kept his eyes shut for the moment.

"You'm sure he baint dead, Missie?"

"Yes," said Sally. "You can see. His face is the proper colour now."

"Ah, he's a brave one to call a storm like that. I never seed our own weatherman do the like, not living so near the Nigromancer as we be. It's surely taxed un."

"It always does," said a voice like a parson's. "You say he's a bit simple, young lady?"

"No, I didn't. He's quite as clever as me or you, only he can't talk and sometimes he looks a bit moony."

"Did you see no one in the wicked machine then?" asked one of the rustic voices. "We did get word as how there was two demons a-driving of it, spitting sparks and all."

"They been hunting un," said another peasant, "all along up from Hungerford way. Lord Willoughby seed un out hawking and give the word. And they damn near caught un last night, I do hear."

"Only she go so mortal fast."

"Hello," said the parsony voice. "I think he's stirring."

Geoffrey sat up, groaned and looked round him. There were more people round than he'd expected, mostly tanned haymakers, but also an oldish man in a long blue cloak with an amber pendant round his neck. Down on the concrete the superb car reproached him with smouldering, stinking wreckage. He smiled at it, what he hoped was a pleased, idiot smile.

"Yes, Jeff," cooed Sal. "You did that. You *are* a clever boy."

He stood up and shifted from foot to foot as the people stared at him. "Please," said Sally, "could you all go away? I don't want him to have one of his fits. It's all right, Jeff. It's all right. Everybody likes you. You're a good boy."

Geoffrey sat down and hid his face in his hands.

One of the rustic voices said, "S'pose we better be getting back along of the hayfield then. Sure you be all right, Missie? We owe you sommat, sort of."

"No thank you, honestly. We don't want anything."

"You get along, chaps; I'll set them on their road and see that they're properly treated." This was the parsony voice. Then there was a diminishing noise of legs swishing through grass, and silence.

"You made a mistake there, young lady. If he'd really made the thunderstorm you'd have asked for money, but of course he didn't have anything to do with it. He might have made that funny little bit of wind from the south-west, but the storm came from the Necromancer, or I'm a Dutchman."

"I wish you'd go away," said Sally. "We're quite all right, really."

"Come, come, young lady. I have only to go and tell those peasants in the hayfield that I can see what looks like a spot of engine oil on our dumb friend's trousers, and then where would you be? Can he talk, as a matter of interest?"

"Yes," said Geoffrey.

"That's more like it," said the man in the blue robe, sitting down beside them and gazing down the embankment.

"What was it?" he asked. "Something pretty primitive, by the look of it."

"A 1909 Silver Ghost," said Geoffrey, nearly crying.

"Dear, dear," said the man. "What a pity. There can't be many of those left. And where were you making for?"

Geoffrey peered at the horizon, working out in his mind the curve of the thundercloud's path in relation to the hills. He pointed.

"Curious," said the man. "So am I. A pity we have no map. I was coming up from the south when I first sensed the storm, and you were coming from the north-east. We could do some crude triangulation with a map, but the point is academic. It would have saved us a deal of trouble."

"I *have* got a map," said Sally, "but I don't know how far it goes. I was still holding it when we got out of the car, but I hid it under my frock when we heard people coming."

"Oh, how perfectly splendid," said the man. "You stay up on the bank and keep cave, young lady, while my colleague and I do our calculations down here out of sight."

As he moved down, Geoffrey saw a gold glint beneath the blue robe.

"Are you a weatherman, too?" he asked.

"At your service, dear colleague."

"Are you the local chap? Did you make the storm?"

"Alas, I am, like yourselves, a wanderer. And also too, it is beyond even my powers to make such a storm as that – though I should certainly have claimed the credit for it had I arrived on the scene in time, and profited more from it than you did. You are something of a traitor to the Guild, dear colleague, refusing fees; but we will mention it no more."

"I thought weathermongers stayed in one place and made weather there. What are you doing wandering about?"

"I might ask the same of you, dear colleague, and even more cogently. Your circumstances are dangerously peculiar. Why did you leave your own source of income, wherever it was?"

"Weymouth. I can't remember much about it, actually, because they hit me on the head, but when I woke up they were trying to drown me and Sal for being witches."

"Ah. They were trying to hang me in Norwich."

"For being a witch too?"

"No, no. For being a businessman. It had long seemed to me that the obese burghers of East Anglia did not adequately appreciate my services, so I announced that I proposed to raise my fees. Of course they refused to play, so to bring them to their senses I made a thunderstorm over Norwich and kept it there for three weeks at the height of the harvest. Unfortunately I had misjudged their temper, and when I heard the citizens come whooping down my street it was not, as I hoped for a moment, to yield to my reasonable demands but to stretch my neck. I left."

"And why do you want to go to Wales?"

"Doubtless for the same reason as yourself. But no, you are too young. You go to find out, do you not?"

"Yes, I suppose so."

"And so, in a way, do I. In my journeyings after leaving Norwich – and let me advise you, young man, that folk do not welcome two weathermongers in a district, and still less does the operator already in possession – in my journeyings I began to hear talk of the Necromancer, subdued talk round inn fires when men had a quart or two of ale in them. Ignorant country gossip, of course, and full of absurdities, but pointing always, and especially as one drew westward, to a source of power in the Welsh hills.

"Yes, that's what we heard," said Geoffrey.

"No doubt. Now, if I am to return to my easy life – oh, so much more agreeable than my old trade of schoolmastering – I need power, power to oust a local weathermonger in some fat district, power more than lies in a mere chivvying of clouds. Some such thing is hidden just over that horizon, and I mean to find it if I can. There is gold in them thar hills, pardner. Let us study the providential map."

It was a one-inch survey, still crackling new, which they spread on the bank, banging it to make it lie level on the grasses.

"H'm, less providential than I thought. You must have been coming almost directly towards the source, and my poor legs do not carry me fast enough to make much difference. I fear we shall have a very narrow base for our triangle."

"Well," said Geoffrey, "we were up here when I first felt it, and about here when I really saw it. It brewed up a little south of west, beyond the north slope of a biggish hill, this one I think. My line runs like this."

"Ah, more useful than I had feared. I had not realised that the motorway curved north as it does, and I had forgotten how fast a motor vehicle can travel. Now, if I lay my line along here, where does that carry us to? Off the map. No, not quite. This is a painfully crude method of measuring, which would not have satisfied me when I had the pleasure of instructing the young in mathematics, but if we were to head for Ewyas Harold we would certainly be going in the right direction, though our destination must be a step or two beyond that."

"It looks an awfully long way, without a car. You don't seem to mind about the car."

"I went through a period," said the weatherman, "Of revulsion from machines, but it has passed. Still, it is not safe to say so, though I suspect that there are more of us about than care to admit it. Certainly, the Black Mountains are a tidy step."

"The thing is I don't know whether Sal is up to it. Couldn't we buy horses?"

"No doubt, given the wherewithal. I myself, I regret to admit, am in somewhat reduced circumstances, but if you have the equivalent of nine gold pieces on you I daresay we could purchase nags of a sort. It would not be money wasted. A horse that can be bought can always be sold again."

"I've got some money."

"Then let us be moving. We will eschew Ross-on-Wye. Townspeople ask tiresome questions of strangers. Which do you think is the better way round?"

"Look, we could head up here through Brampton Abbots, then jiggle down to the railway line and over to Sellack. Then, if we take this footpath we can cut through along the river bank here and get on to this road which runs all the way to Ewyas Harold."

"That will do passably well," said the weatherman. "*Marchons mes enfants.* Good heavens, what a pleasure it is to be able to speak in a civilised manner after all these years. But we must be cautious. I think, dear colleague, that you had best revert to the dumb idiocy which you portrayed so convincingly to the yokels a while back. You might well be my servant. A leech – I usually travel in the guise of a leech, and do less harm than most of the profession – might well have picked up some poor creature brought to him for cure. I think, however, that we will not afflict the young lady with loss of speech – the strain would be too great for her. She shall be my ward, and as such should call me Dominus. Do you know Latin, young lady?"

"Yes," said Sally. "I'm hungry, and where are we going to sleep?"

"You shall eat at the first likely farm, while I haggle for a horse. We are unlikely to pick up more than one at any one place, because horses are still scarce, now that the tractors are no more. Big farm horses command huge sums, but there is a plethora of ponies left behind by the pony clubs. We shall contrive something before dusk, I doubt not. Perhaps it would be more verisimilitudinous if Geoffrey were to disburse what coin I am likely to need while we are still hidden. It would not do for me to have to ask my servant for gold."

Geoffrey brought out his purse and gave the weatherman ten gold pieces. He still felt dazed, and was glad after the hideous careering and decision taking to put himself into the hands of this self-assured adult. He felt hungry too. They had breakfasted at dawn and missed lunch, and the world was now heaving over towards evening. At least they ought to be sure of a fine night, with two weathermen on the staff, if it came to sleeping out.

They crossed the motorway, not looking at the ruined Rolls. Up on the other side, a field away, lay a small road along which they walked slowly, sending up puffs of summer dust at every step. Sally seemed very tired, her face drawn and sullen, mouth drooping, skin grey beneath the dirt and tan. In a mile they found a cottage beside the road where the weatherman, leaning on his staff, sent Geoffrey to knock on the door. A mild old dame, stained beyond the wrists with blackcurrant juice, came out into the sunlight and answered the weatherman's imperious questions. Yes, she knew for sure that Mr Grindall up at Overton had a roan foal for sale. He'd taken it to Ross Market only last week but hadn't been offered a price. And mebbe he had another. And at Park Farm they might have horses to spare. Folk were afeard, living so close to the Nigromancer, and there wasn't always men to work the horses. They'd all gone east, to easier climes, including her own two sons, and times were terrible hard...

The voice trailed away into a whining snivel. Unmoved, the weatherman stared at her, as if she were telling him lies, until she hauled up her long black skirts and scuttled back into the cottage.

"We must move on a few paces," he said in a low voice, "so that we may look at the map unseen and hope that Overton is on it."

"It's up that track there," whispered Geoffrey, back to the cottage. "I remember from the map. And Park Farm's a bit beyond it."

"What! Total recall! I have always regarded it as an obscene myth. Still, I must take advantage of your faculties just as you must take advantage of mine – social contract, in effect. Rousseau *would* have been pleased."

At Overton Farm the weatherman's demeanour was completely different. He became soft and smooth, rubbing his hands together and cooing at the girl who opened the door, and then at the sturdy farmhouse wife who pushed her aside. He was a leech from Gloucester, he said, hasting north at the command of my Lord Salting, to attend the birth of an heir. Now they were late, having stayed by the way to succour a village oppressed with a running sickness. They were tired and hungry. Could they rest awhile and buy milk and bread? And if by chance there were any illness in the house he would be glad to do what he could in recompense for hospitality.

The farmwife led them indoors to a room where the pattern of embossed wallpaper still showed through white distemper. The fireplace had undergone an upheaval in order to install a great open range, unlit at this time of year, with hooks for curing hams in the chimney and a bread oven jutting across the hearth beside it. The furniture was hard oak, crudely made. Sally and the weatherman sat on a long bench and Geoffrey stood against the wall, pulling faces at random to sustain his reputation for idiocy, while the farmwife and her maid clattered in the scullery beyond.

His dizziness was gone, and he was beginning to have doubts about the weatherman. There was something too slick about him, and he really had been horrid to the poor old woman at the cottage. But he did know his way about. He was being very useful now, and rather cunning not mentioning horses at all.

The farmwife came back with a leg of cold mutton, and the maid brought ale, milk, butter and rough brown bread. They ate for a while in silence, but soon the farmwife started asking where they'd come from and why they hadn't gone through Ross. She didn't sound suspicious, just curious, and the weatherman satisfied her by saying that Geoffrey tended to have fits in towns. They all sighed and glanced at him, and to keep them happy he pulled another face. Then the weatherman asked about crossing the Wye, and was told to take the path down to the old railway bridge, keeping an eye open for thunderstorms in case the Nigromancer chose to throw a bolt at it. It was only at this point that he mentioned horses, in the most casual way, as though he wasn't really interested and honestly preferred walking. It was just that they were so late for this important birth, and his lordship was not a man to displease. The farmwife's face turned hard and greedy and she called to the maid to go and fetch the master from the cow byre.

He was a small, dark, beaten-looking man, and even when he was there his wife did most of the talking, speaking of the superexcellent quality of the farm's horses, and how exceedingly lucky the travellers were that there should be, at this moment, not one but two to spare, which were a bargain at seven sovereigns. The weatherman nodded and smiled until the two horses were led into the yard. One was a lean, tall roan and the other a restless piebald. The weatherman grunted and strolled over to them, feeling their legs and sides, forcing their mouths open, banging their shoulders. At last he stood up, shook his head and offered the farmwife three sovereigns for the pair, or four with harness thrown in. At once there was a cackle of dismay, as if a fox had got into a henhouse, and they settled down to hard bargaining, with the weatherman holding the upper ground, as he could claim both that they didn't really want horses and also that two horses were no good to them in any case – they really wanted three.

The haggling grumbled back and forth, like a slow-motion game of tennis, until the farmer broke into a pause.

"If you be wanting three horses," he said, "we got a pony as might do for the young lady. He's a liddle 'un, but he's a good 'un."

He shambled off round the corner of a barn and returned with the most extraordinary animal, a hairy, square thing with four short legs under it, dark brown, the texture of a doormat, with a black mane and a sulky eye. It snarled at the people, and when the weatherman was feeling its hocks it chose its moment and bit him hard in the fleshy part of the thigh. He jumped back, his face black with rage.

"Ah," said the farmer, "you want to watch un. He's strong, but he's wilful. Tell you what, you take the other two for five-an-a-narf sov, an' I'll give un to you, saddle an' all. Ach, shut up, Madge. He eats more than he's worth every month, an' *we've* no use for un."

The weatherman rubbed his thigh, pulled his temper together and looked at Sally.

"What do you think, my dear," he said. "Can you manage him? He gave me a vicious nip."

"What's his name?" said Sally.

"Maddox," said the farmer. "I dunno why."

Sally felt in a pocket of her blouse and brought out a small orange cube. Geoffrey recognised it at once by the smell: it was a piece of the gipsy's horse-bait. She broke it in half and walked stolidly towards the pony, holding a fragment in the flat of her palm. The other two horses edged in towards the sweet, treacly smell.

"Keep them away," said Sally. "This is for Maddox. Come on then, boy. Come on. That's a nice Maddox. Come on. There. Now, if you're a good pony and do what I tell you, you shall have the other half for your supper. You *are* a good pony. I know you are."

She scratched as hard as she could through the doormat hair between his ears, and he nuzzled in to her side, nearly knocking her over, looking for the rest of the horse-bait.

"Well," said the farmer, "I never seed anything like

it. I'll just nip off and fetch his harness afore he changes his mind. Five-an-a-narf sov it is then, mister?"

"I suppose so," said the weatherman, and counted the money out into the farmwife's hand. She bit every coin.

The horses jibbed at the railway bridge, disturbed by the machine-forged metal, until Sally led Maddox up on to the causeway and the other two followed. It really was evening now, a world of soft, warm gold, with the hedge trees black on their sunless side and casting field-wide shadows. They plugged on (Geoffrey very unhappy on the piebald) through Sellack, along the path by the river bank on to the road again near Kynaston, and up the slow westward hill. It was almost dark, with Sally yawning and swaying in her saddle, before the weatherman agreed to stop for the night.

The place he chose wasn't bad, a disused huddle of farm buildings backing on to a field which was a wild tangle of weeds and self-sown wheat. There was a big Dutch barn of corrugated asbestos, half its roof blown off in some freak wind, but filled with rusting tractors, combines, balers, hoists and such. It didn't look as though they'd been afflicted by any special visitations from over the horizon, no such holocaust as had destroyed the Rolls. Given time and petrol,

Geoffrey felt that he could have got some of them to go. But the moment a cylinder stirred, the wrath of the Necromancer would be down on them.

They ate and slept in another barn, floored with musty straw. The weatherman had bought bread and walletful of mutton at the farm, and they sat with their backs against decaying bales and munched and talked. Sally, curiously, did most of the talking – about life in Weymouth, and the respect Geoffrey was held in, and the inadequacy of other Dorset weathermen compared to him. When the weatherman spoke he did so in smooth, rolling clauses, full of long words such as schoolmasters use when they are teasing a favoured pupil, but he told them very little about himself. His talk was like candyfloss, that huge sweet bauble that fills the eye but leaves little in your belly when you've eaten it. At last he gave them both a nip of liquor from a flask "to help them sleep", and they wormed themselves into the powdery straw, disturbed by tickling fragments at first, then cosy with generated warmth, then miles deep in the chasms of sleep.

When they woke in the morning the weatherman was gone, and so was the roan, and so was Geoffrey's purse.

8

THE TOWER

He had left the piebald horse and Maddox. Also a
square of red cloth containing some bread and mutton
and a letter.

Dear Colleague,
  I know you will understand when I tell you that I
have changed my mind. I am not really (as you so
evidently are) the stuff of which high adventures
are made. So, learning that there was a decent
billet for a weathermonger of my abilities at
Weymouth, I realised that it ill became me to
deprive you of a share in the honour and glory (if

any). You have but twenty miles to go, while I have half a country. I was sure (and therefore decided that it was kindest not to wake you) that you would, in the circumstances, have pressed upon me a loan which it would have been embarrassing to refuse. If the burghers of Weymouth are as free with their money as your sister implies, I shall be in a position to repay you the next time you pass that way, when no doubt we shall have much to talk about.

Meanwhile I remain

Your devoted admirer

CYRIL CAMPERDOWN

(not, of course, my real name)

PS You should be able to sell the piebald for two sovs (ask three) provided you don't let the purchaser inspect his off hind foot. Maddox might be edible, stewed very slowly for several hours.

Sally said, "He never liked poor Maddox, not since he bit him."

Geoffrey said, "What are we going to do?"

"What he says, I think, except for eating Maddox. If it's really only twenty miles, we could sell your horse and take turns to ride Maddox, and we ought to be there for supper."

"And what then?"

"Oh, Jeff, I don't think that's a very sensible question. Absolutely anything might happen, so there's no point in thinking about it, like you said last night. I think we've done jolly well to get as far as we have done, honestly."

"I expect you're right."

He felt muddled by the weatherman's treachery – sorry that somebody who he'd liked and who had been helpful should turn out such a stinker; glad to be on their own again. They ate the bread and mutton and decided on a story – Sally couldn't cope with Geoffrey remaining officially dumb. It seemed easiest to stick to the weatherman's basic lie, simply adding that they'd been sent ahead but had missed their master on the road and had to sell the piebald to get home.

This worked surprisingly well. The first farm they tried didn't want another horse, but gave them each a mug of milk for nothing. The second was full of squalling dogs so they gave it a miss. But at the third the farmer seemed interested. Geoffrey held the piebald and Sally kept Maddox as close to the suspect foot as she could. The farmer went through the ritual of prodding and feeling, but when he came round to the off hind quarter and bent down Sally gave Maddox a bit more rope and he lunged and bit the farmer's ear. The man swore. Geoffrey apologised and spoke crossly to Sally. The farmer's wife leaned out of an upstairs window and jeered at him. He didn't seem to fancy any more feelings and prodding, but took the horse for two and a half sovereigns.

It turned out that Maddox wouldn't let Geoffrey ride him, even with Sally leading. This suited Geoffrey very well, as it allowed Sally to ride and rest (it wasn't like real riding – no bumpity-bumpity – more like travelling on a coarse, swaying sofa) while he walked beside her. The pony's pace exactly matched his, and they ambled west in a mood extraordinarily different from yesterday's. Then they had felt invaders, alien, blasting their way between the growing greens of early harvest; now they were part of the scenery, moving at a pace natural to their surroundings. Haymakers straightened from scythes and waved to them, shouting incomprehensible good-days. For two miles, between Orcop and Bagwy Llydiart, they walked with a girl of about Geoffrey's age, a plump, bun-faced lass who talked to them in a single incessant stream of lilting language – about her relations and acquaintances, never pausing to explain who anybody was, but assuming that they both knew Cousin William and Mr Price and Poor Old John as well as she did. The idea that anybody really lived outside the span of the immediate horizon – closer now as the foothills of Wales grew steeper – was clearly beyond her. Two or three times she referred casually to the presence of the Nigromancer, twelve miles westward, as one might refer to the existence of a river at the bottom of the paddock – a natural hazard that must be reckoned with but which nothing in the ordinary round of life could affect or change. Listening to her with less than half of his mind, Geoffrey found himself thinking about the General and his missiles. He had only the vaguest idea about these weapons, but he was fairly certain that they could not be guaranteed to land, pat, on the spot they were aimed at. Twelve miles off target wasn't much in a trajectory that length, and then there'd be no bun-faced girl striding along a lane and prattling about Cousin William.

She left them before Bagwy Llydiart, in mid-sentence. Geoffrey and Sally got the subject and verb, and the girl who opened the farm door to her got the object.

In the village, which was really only an inn and a couple of houses, they bought bread and bacon and cider. Geoffrey had been rehearsing his story for the last half mile up the hill, but found it wasn't needed. The bar had five old men in it, all talking eagerly about the demon-driven engine which had been slain on the bad road by a storm from over the mountains. The accounts of the two demons were exciting but confusing, because two different stories seemed to have arrived in the village together. In one the car had been driven by monsters, horned, warty, blowing flames from their noses; in the other by a man and woman of surpassing but devilish beauty. Both stories agreed that no remains had been found in the car, which made the supernatural quality of the drivers obvious. Then the landlord joined in the talk, after doing complicated sums with Geoffrey's change – England seemed to have some very peculiar coins these days.

"I did hear," he said, "as how Lord Willoughby had hunted un all the way up from Hungerford, and precious near caught un last night. And they'm sending South for his lordship's hounds, as may still have the scent in 'em, after nosing round where the engine stopped in the dark. *I* don't reckon 'em for demons. What need would there be for the likes of demons to go stopping in the dark? You mark my words – they was nobbut wicked outlanders, who seed the storm a-coming and left their engine in time. S'posing his lordship brings the dogs up in coaches, they'll be on the bad road two hours since. Then there'll be fine hunting."

"Lot o' s'posin's," said one of the old drinkers. "They'm demons for my money."

The argument circled back on to its old track, and Geoffrey left, sick with panic. Fifteen miles start, perhaps, and there'd been a good stretch yesterday evening when everyone was riding. That should confuse them. On the other hand the hunt must have guessed where they were making for by now, and once they'd been traced to Overton Farm there'd be descriptions available, of a sort.

Sally had become bored with waiting, and was trying to balance, standing, like a circus rider, on Maddox's back. It can't have been difficult on the broad plateau of his shoulders, but she looked nervous and sat down the moment she saw Geoffrey.

"What's the matter?" she whispered.

"Nothing. I hope."

"Oh, you must tell me. It isn't fair being left in the dark."

"Something they said in the pub. It looks as if we're still being hunted by those hounds."

"Oh bother. Just when everything seemed so easy and right. What are you going to do?"

"I don't know. Plug on, I suppose. They can hunt us wherever we go, you see."

"I suppose perhaps if we got close enough to the nigro man they might be too frightened to follow us."

"It's a chance – the best one probably."

"I wonder if they'll start hunting our weatherman too. That would surprise him."

Indeed it might, but no doubt he'd talk his way out of it. Geoffrey decided not to stop for lunch but to eat walking. Maddox decided otherwise, and won. They ate their bacon (smoked, not salted, and very fatty) and drank their sweet unbubbly cider a mile out of the village, where the hill sloped gently down in front of them. Maddox found a stretch of grass which appealed to him and champed stolidly. Geoffrey and Sally sat on the gate of an overgrown orchard and looked west. Now, for the first time, they could see how close the ramparts of the Black Mountains loomed, a dark, hard-edged frame to the green and loping landscape. Nothing on the near side of the escarpment looked at all peculiar. The haymakers were at work as they had been in Wiltshire; an old woman in a black dress, leading a single cow, came up the road towards them and gave them good-day. Perhaps fewer of the fields were worked here, and more had been let go, but that might be simply because the soil here was less rewarding than in the counties they had passed through yesterday. You couldn't tell.

Maddox took nearly an hour to finish his meal. Without event they covered the long drop into Pontrilas, where they crossed the Monnow and found a two-mile footpath up to Rowlstone. Here the country grew much steeper, so that Geoffrey realised how tired his hams were, and that there was a blister coming on his left heel. On the crest of Mynydd Merddin they rested and looked back.

"See anything, Sal?"

"No. They couldn't be coming yet, could they?"

"Not unless they were dead lucky. We ought to have three or four hours yet. What we really need is a stream going roughly the way we want to go, and then wade down it, but there doesn't look as if there's anything right on the map. This one at the bottom's too big, I think. On we go."

Clodock, in the valley, was an empty village with its

church in ruins, but the bridge still stood. The mountains heeled above them. Geoffrey led Maddox up a footpath, very disused and overgrown, to Penyrhiwiau, where the track turned left and lanced straight towards the ramparts. Already it was steeper than anything they'd climbed, and the contour lines on the map showed there was worse to come. The hills were silent, a bare, untenanted upheaval of sour soil covered with spiky brown grass and heather. He'd been expecting to see mountain sheep and half-wild ponies, but not an animal seemed to move between horizon and horizon, not even a bird. He felt oppressed by their total loneliness, and thought Sally did too. Only Maddox plodded on unmoved.

His heart was banging like an iron machine and his lungs sucking in air and shoving it out in quick, harsh panting, like a dog's, when they took the path south-west for the final climb. This path slanted sideways up the hill, so that they could look out to the left over the prodigious summer landscape. No road could have taken that hill direct; it must have been one in one, and was topped, besides, with a line of low cliffs, where the underlying bone of the hills showed through the weather-worn flesh. Their path slanted round the end of these and then (the map said) turned sharply back, down through terrain just as bleak to Llanthony. It looked as though there was a stream they could wade down starting almost on the far path. His legs were too accustomed, by now, to the rhythm of hurrying to move at a slower pace, but when they rounded the cliff at the top he knew that he had to rest.

Sally slid off Maddox and lay on the grass beside him, looking back over their route. The pony nosed disgustedly among the coarse grass for something worthy of his palate. Geoffrey swung the map round and tried to work out exactly where they'd been. Mynydd Merddin seemed no more than a gentle swelling out of the plain, until you realised for how far it hid the country behind it. Then that must be their path, coming down by the tip of that wood, and into Clodock, which was easy to spot by its square church tower. Of course he would not be able to see the footpath from here – it had been so overgrown that...

He *could* see it. Not the path itself, of course, but the horsemen on it. And, in a gap, the wavering pale line which was the backs of hounds.

He stared at them hopelessly.

"Come on, Jeff. We can't give up now, after getting so far. Do come on."

He shambled up the path, too tired to run, to the crest of the hill. Perhaps he'd be able to run a bit down the far side; then, if they could get to the stream, or at least if he could send Sal off down it, there might be hope. Eyes on the track, he weltered on.

"Oh!" cried Sally, and he looked up.

They were on the crest, and the Valley of Ewyas lay beneath them. It was quite crazy. Instead of the acid, barren hills that should have been there, he saw a forest of enormous trees beginning not fifty yards down the slope with no outlying scrub or thicket to screen the grey, centuries-old trunks. Beneath the leaves, beyond the trunks, lay shadows blacker than any wood he had ever seen. Above, reaching north and south and out of eyesight, the green cumulus obliterated the valley. Out of the middle of it, a single monstrous tower, rose the Necromancer's Castle. It could be nothing else. Their path led into the wood and straight towards it.

9

THE SENESCHAL

A crooked tissue of wind brought the sound of hallooing from over the cliffs behind them.

"Come on," said Sally, "it's the best bet. Maddox, you're going to have to see if you can go a bit faster."

With the help of the downward slope the pony managed to produce out of his repertoire a long-forgotten trot. In a way he was like the Rolls, a rectangular, solid, unstoppable thing. Geoffrey, now in a daze of tiredness, let the path take him down it in a freewheeling lope, which he knew would end in fainting limpness the moment the path flattened to a level. They plunged into the trees.

It was darker than he'd thought possible. This was a quite different sort of forest from the gone-to-pot New Forest which they'd breakfasted in yesterday. That had seemed, somehow, like a neglected grove at the bottom of a big garden – after all, its trees had been tended like a vegetable crop only six years before. But this one had not seen a forester's axe for generations of trees. The oaks were prodigious, their trunks fuzzy with moss, and the underwoods were a striving, rotting tangle, tall enough to overarch the path for most of the way – this was what made the shadows so dark. The silence was thick, ominous, complete; even the noise of Maddox's hooves was muffled by the moss on which they ran, a soft, deep, dark-green pile which would surely be worn away in no time if the road was used much – used at all. Why had the forest not swallowed it? It lay broad as a carriageway between the tree trunks, without even a bramble stretching across it.

"Jeff, what was that?"

"What?"

"That. Listen."

A noise of dogs howling. The hunt, of course. But it came from the wrong direction, forwards and to their right, and was different from the baying they'd heard last night – deeper, more intense, wilder.

"Jeff, there aren't any *wolves* in England today, are there?"

"I hope not. But anything—"

There it was again. No, that *was* the hunt this time, behind them and distinctly shriller – they must be at the crest now. The new noise welled up again, closer, but still to their right, up the hill, and the hunt behind them bayed its answer. And here, at last, was the stream.

"Look, Sal, this is the only hope. Get off and lead Maddox down there, keeping in the water. I'll run down here a bit further and then come back. Keep going down the stream till I catch up with you."

"You *will* come back won't you? Promise."

"All right."

"Promise."

"I promise."

She led Maddox gingerly into the stream, which was steep and stony, and Geoffrey pounded on down the mossy ride. He thought at once that he ought to have brought Maddox too, and bolted him on downwards while he climbed back to the scent-obliterating water, except that Maddox wasn't the sort to fit into elaborate schemes of deception. Hurrah, here was another stream, too small to be marked on the map; if he went back now the hunt might waste time exploring this one.

The climb seemed like a crawl, and the woods swayed round him. This was hopeless – he must have somehow branched on to another path without noticing – there wasn't a sign of his footprints on the moss. He looked back, and saw that he'd left no track there either, which would help the deception supposing he got back to the first stream on time. The two choruses of baying clashed out at each other again, and the hunt sounded fearfully close. At last he splashed down into the stream, his weak legs treacherous on the wobbly boulders, and waded downstream. He caught Sally up only a few bends down.

"You ought to have got further. You shouldn't have waited."

"I didn't, but Maddox felt thirsty. Come on now, boy. Not far. Oh!"

Her quack of surprise was almost inaudible in the yelping and baying that shook the wood. Somewhere on the path the two packs must have met. Above the clamour he could hear human voices shouting and cursing; they did not sound as if they were in control of the situation.

He followed Sally down to a lower road, which also seemed to lead towards the tower; without a word they turned off along it, padding in a haze of silence down the endless mossy avenue while the battle in the woods above them whimpered into stillness. He realised with surprise that the darkness was not only caused by the double roofing of leaves; it was drawing towards night outside, and the tower, whatever it might hold, was the only chance of escaping from the fanged things that ranged these woods. And at least they would have arrived, against all odds, at the target at which the General had aimed them three whole days ago in Morlaix. And he hadn't had a proper sleep since then. A voice somewhere, confused by the booming in his ears, started saying "Poor old Jeff. Poor old Jeff," over and over again. It was his own.

He was drowning in self-pity when they stepped out of the forest into the clearing round the tower. It was enormous, three times as high as the giant trees, wide as a tithe barn, a piled circle of rough-hewn masonry sloping steadily in towards the top – the same shape as those crude stone towers which the Celts built two thousand years ago in the Shetland Islands, but paralysingly larger. Round its base, some distance away from it, ran a stone skirting wall about as high as an ordinary house. Just outside this was a deep dry ditch, and then the clearing they stood in. There was no door or window in this side of the wall, so they turned left, downhill, looking up at the monstrous pillar of stonework in the centre with a few stars coming out behind its level summit. The black wood brooded on their left.

They rounded a sharper curve by the ditch, and saw the line of wall interrupted. Eighty yards on was a bridge across the dry moat, and two small turrets set into the wall. As they trudged through the clinging grasses towards it no sound came from the tower, no light showed. Perhaps it was empty. They crossed the bridge and found the gate shut. Geoffrey hammered at it with his fist, but made no more noise than snow on a window pane. He crossed the bridge again to look for a stone to hammer with, but Sally pointed above their heads.

At first he thought there was a single huge fruit hanging from the tree above the path, then he realised it was too big even for that, and decided it must be a hornet's nest. He moved and the round thinned. When he was under it it looked like a thick plate, something man-made.

"What is it, Sal?"

"I think it's a gong. You come along here on your charger and bonk it with your lance and the lord of the castle comes out to answer your challenge. If you stood on Maddox's back you might be able to reach it. Come here, Maddox. That's a good boy. Up you get, Jeff. Oh, Maddox, you are *awful*. I'll see if I've got any horse-bait left. Here. Stand still. That's right. Now Jeff!"

He scrambled on to the broad back. The gong was just above his head and he struck at it with the fat edge of his fist. It made a tremendous noise, a sustained boom that died away at last into curious whinings all the way up the diapason. Nothing stirred in the tower. He struck the gong several times, judging its internal rhythm so that each blow produced a louder boom. At last Maddox decided that enough was enough and shied away; Geoffrey slithered down and the three of them stood listening to the resonance of bronze diminish into whimperings.

In the new silence they realised they could hear another noise, one that they had heard several times that afternoon. The baying of wolves (or whatever they were) was echoing through the valley, seeming to come at times from all round the compass, but at other times from the hill they had themselves descended. It was getting nearer.

"Jeff! D'you think we ought to go on?"

"We'll give it another minute and then we'll climb a tree. Maddox will have to... Look!"

In the near-dark they could see a movement of light behind the postern tower. A few seconds later they heard a rattle of chains and the grate of rusty metal drawn through metal. In the big gate a small door started to open and they ran towards it. A face thrust through, with a long white beard waggling beneath it.

"Well," said the face, "what is it? Do you realise how late it is? I was just shutting up."

"Please," said Sally, "but we got lost in the wood and it seems to be full of wolves or something and could we come in for the night, please?"

"Ah," said the face, "benighted travellers. Yes, yes, I'm sure he would think that proper, as far as one can be sure of anything. Come in. Goodness me, what an extraordinary animal! Is it a dog or a horse? Oh, it's a pony, according to its lights. Well, well. Come in."

The small door swung wide open, so that they could see his whole body. He was a little, bent man, holding a flaming branch which had been soaked in some sort of tar or resin which made it flare in the dark. He wore sweeping velvet robes, trimmed with ermine round the edges; a soft velvet cap, patterned with pearls and gold thread, sloped down the side of his head. Sally led Maddox in, and as Geoffrey stepped over the threshold there was a snarling in the trees and a pack of dark shapes with gleaming eyes came swirling towards the door. The little man pushed it almost shut, poked his head out again and said, "Shoo! Shoo! Be off with you! Shoo!"

He shut the door completely, pushed two large bolts across, swung a huge balanced beam into slots so that it barred the whole gateway and laced several chains into position over it.

"Nasty brutes," he said, "but they're all right if you speak to them firmly. This way. We'll put your animal into the stables and then we'll go and see if there's anything for dinner. I expect you'll be hungry. Do you know, you're really our first visitors. I think he doesn't fancy the idea of people prying around, reporters from the newspapers, you know, which is why he put the wolves there. But benighted travellers is quite different – I think he'll appreciate that – it's so romantic, and that's what he seems to like, as you can see."

He waved a vague arm at the colossal tower, and led them into a long shed which leant against the outer wall. It was crudely partitioned into stalls.

"Tie him up anywhere," said the old man. "There ought to be oats in one of those bins, and you can draw water from the well."

"Poor Maddox," said Sally, looking down the empty length of stables, where black shadows jumped about in the wavering flare of the torch, "I'm afraid you're going to feel lonely."

"Oh, you can't tell," said their host. "Really you can't. Having one pony here might put ideas into his head, and then we'd wake up to find the whole place full of horses, all needing watering and feeding. I don't think he has any idea of the work involved, keeping a place like this going, but then he doesn't have to."

The bins were all brimming with grain, and there was sweet fresh hay in a barn next door. Geoffrey worked the windlass of the well, and found that the water was only a few feet down. They left Maddox tucking in to a full manger, like a worn traveller who, against all the odds, has finished up at a five-star hotel. As they crossed the courtyard to the keep they realised it was now full night, the sky pied with huge stars and a chill night breeze creeping up the valley. The door to the keep was black oak, a foot thick, tall as a haystack. The old man levered it open with a pointed pole. Geoffrey noticed that it could be barred both inside and out.

Beyond the door lay a single circular chamber, with a fire in the middle. It was sixty foot from where they stood to the fire, and sixty foot on to the far wall. The fire was big as a Guy Fawkes bonfire, piled with trunks of trees, throwing orange light and spitting sparks across the rush-strewn paving stones. Round it slept a horde of rangy, woolly dogs, each almost as large as Maddox. The smoke filled the roof beams and made its way out through a hole in the centre of the roof, which, Geoffrey realised, high though it seemed, cannot have come more than a third of the way up the tower. He wondered what lay above. Round the outside wall of the chamber, ten feet above the floor, ran a wide wooden gallery supported on black oak pillars. It reached up to the roof, with two rows of unglazed windows looking out across the chamber. Beneath the gallery, against the wall, stood a line of flaring torches, like the one the old man carried, in iron brackets. Between them pot-shaped helmets gleamed. On either side of the fire, reaching towards them, ran two long black tables, piled high with great hummocks of food, meat and pastry and fruits, with plates and goblets scattered down their length and low benches ranged beneath the tables. They walked up towards the fire between an avenue of eatables.

"Oh, splendid!" exclaimed the old man. "Perhaps he heard the gong and decided it was time for a feast. Often he doesn't think about food for days and days, you know, and then it starts to go bad and I have to throw it out to the wolves – I used to have such a nice little bird table at my own house – and I don't know which way to turn really I don't. Now, let's see. If you sit there, and you there, I'll sit in the middle and carve. I suppose we ought to introduce ourselves. My name's Willoughby Furbelow and I'm Seneschal of the castle."

"I'm Geoffrey Tinker and this is my sister Sally. It's very kind of you to put us up."

"Not at all, not at all. That's what I'm here for, I suppose, though it isn't at all what I intended. Really this place ought to be full of wandering minstrels and chance-come guests and thanes riding in to pay homage and that sort of thing, only they don't seem to come. Perhaps it's the wolves that put them off, or else you're all too busy out there in the big world. I keep trying to tell him he ought to do something about the wolves, but he doesn't seem very interested and my Latin isn't very good – I keep having to look things up in the dictionary and I never thought I'd need a grammar when it all started, all those tenses and cases you know, I find them very muddling and he does get terribly *bored*. Or perhaps it's the morphine. Now, this thing here is a boar's head. Actually there isn't a lot of meat on it, and it's a pig to carve (pardon the pun) and though some bits of it are very tasty others aren't, and besides it seems a pity to spoil it just for the three of us, it looks so splendid doesn't it? Would you mind if I suggested we had a go at this chicken? You mustn't mind it looking so yellow. Everything seems to get cooked in saffron, and it really does taste quite nice, though you weary of it after a few years. Which part do you fancy, Miss Trinket, or may I call you Sarah?"

"Everyone calls me Sally and may I have a wing and some breast, please? There don't seem to be any potatoes. And what's that green stuff?"

"Good King Henry. It's a weed really, but it's quite nice, like spinach. I'm afraid they didn't have any potatoes in his day, any more than they had the fish fingers you're used to, but there are probably some wurzels down below the salt, if you fancy them. You do realise you've got to eat all this in your fingers, like a picnic? I used to have such a nice set of fish knives and forks, with mother-of-pearl handles, which my late wife and I were given for a wedding present. I think I miss them as much as anything. But the bread is very nice when it's fresh and you can use it for mopping up gravy and things. There. Now, Geoffrey?"

"Please, may I have a leg? I didn't understand what you said about morphine."

"It wouldn't be safe to stop it, really it wouldn't. Perhaps I should never have started. Things have not turned out at all the way I intended, I promise you. But now... I don't know what would happen if I stopped giving it him. He calls it his 'food', you know. I looked that up. But there'd be the most terrible withdrawal symptoms. He might destroy the whole world, really he might. It says so on his stone. Just think – he built this place in a single night, and all the wood too, and the wolves, in a single night. I often wonder whether he interferes with telly reception outside the valley. But what he would do if he were really upset I don't like to think. Is that enough, or would you like a bit of breast too?"

"That's fine, thanks," said Geoffrey. Mr Furbelow

was one of those men who cannot talk and do anything else at the same time, so Geoffrey's helping had been mangled off somehow between sentences, and then the high, eager, silly voice rambled on. The old man helped himself to several slices of breast and both oysters, and then began to worry about drink.

"Dear me, I don't know what my late wife would say about Sally drinking wine. She was a pillar of the Abergavenny temperance movement. I had a little chemist's shop in Abergavenny, you know. That's what made the whole thing possible. As a chemist, I cannot advise you to drink the water, and though there is mead and ale below the salt, I myself find them very affecting, more so than the wine. I trust you will be moderate."

The chicken was delicious, though almost cold. Geoffrey was still hungry when he had finished and helped himself from a salver of small chops, which were easy to eat in his fingers, unlike the Good King Henry, which had to be scooped up on pieces of dark soft bread. His knife was desperately sharp steel, with a horn handle bound with silver. His plate seemed to be gold, and so did the goblet from which he drank the sweet cough-syrupy wine. All the while Mr Furbelow talked, at first making mysterious references to the "he" who owned the tower and provided the feast, and then, as he filled his own goblet several times more, about the old days in Abergavenny, and a famous trip he and his wife had made in the summer of 1959 to the Costa Brava. It took him a long time to finish his chicken. At last he pushed his plate back, reached for a clean one from the far side of the table and pointed with his knife at an enormous arrangement of pastry, shaped like a castle, with little pastry soldiers marching about on top of it.

"You *could* have some of that, if you liked, but you never know what you'll find inside it. If you fancy a sweet there might be some wild strawberries in that bowl just up there beyond the peacock, Sally dear. Ah, splendid. And fresh cream too. No sugar of course. Now you must tell me something about yourselves. I seem to have done all the talking."

This had been worrying Geoffrey. He didn't know what a seneschal would feel about a travelling leech's dependents. Would he come over snobbish, and send them down below the salt? Or would the chemist from Abergavenny be impressed by the magical title of Doctor?

"Honestly," he said, "there isn't much to say about

us. We're orphans, and we were travelling North with our guardian, who is a leech, when he had to hurry on and help someone have a baby, a lord's wife, I think, and he told us where to meet him but we made a mistake and got lost, and when we heard the wolves in the forest we ran here."

"Dear me," said Mr Furbelow, "I'm afraid your guardian will be worrying about you."

Sally, her mouth full of strawberries, said sulkily, "I don't like our guardian. I think he'd be glad if we were eaten by wolves."

"Oh, Sally, he's been awfully kind to us." (Geoffrey hoped he didn't sound as though he meant it.)

"You said yourself that he couldn't wait to get his hands on the estate. I bet you he doesn't even try to look for us."

"What's a leech?" said Mr Furbelow.

"A doctor."

"Do you mean," said Mr Furbelow, "that this" (he waved a vague hand at the tower and the hounds and the Dark-Ages appurtenances) "goes on outside the valley?"

"Oh, yes," said Geoffrey. "All over England. Didn't you know?"

"I've often wondered," said Mr Furbelow, "but of

course I couldn't go and see. And how did this doctor come to be your guardian?"

"He was a friend of Father's," said Geoffrey, "and when Dad died he left us in his care, so now we have to go galumphing round the country with him and he treats us like servants. I shouldn't have said that."

"You poor things," said Mr Furbelow. "I don't know what to do for the best, honestly I don't. Perhaps you'd better stay here for a bit and keep me company. I'm sure *he* won't mind, and I'll be delighted to have someone to talk to after all these years."

"It's terribly kind of you, sir," said Geoffrey. "I think it would suit us very well. I hope we can do something to help you, but I don't know what."

"Well," said Sally. "*I* can speak Latin!"

Oh lord, thought Geoffrey, that's spoilt everything, just when we were getting on so well. She's tired and had too much wine, and now she's said something he can find out isn't true in no time. Indeed the old man was peering at Sally with a dotty fierceness, and Geoffrey began to look round for a weapon to clock him with if there was trouble.

"Dic mihi," said Mr Furbelow stumblingly, "quid agitis in his montibus."

"Benigne," said Sally. "Magister Carolus, cuius pupilli sumus, medicus notabilis, properabat ad castellum Sudeleianum, qua (ut nuntius ei dixerat) uxor baronis iam iam parturiverit. Nobis imperavit magister..."

"How marvellous," said Mr Furbelow. "I'm afraid I can't follow you at that speed. Did you say Sudeley Castle? I went there once on a coach trip with my late wife; she enjoyed that sort of outing. Oh dear, it *is* late. We must talk about this tomorrow. Now it's really time you were in bed. He might put the torches out suddenly. Perhaps you'd like to share the same room. This castle is a bit frightening for kiddies, I always think."

He said the last bit in a noisy whisper to Geoffrey, and then showed them down to the far wall where a staircase, which was really more like a ladder, led up to the gallery. There were several other ladders like it round the hall. Upstairs they found a long, narrow room, with a large window looking out over the hall and a tiny square one cut into the thickness of the wall. Through this they could see the top of the outer wall, and beyond that a section of forest, black in the moonlight, and beyond that the blacker hills. There were no beds in the room, only oak chests, huge feather mattresses like floppy bolsters, and hundreds of fur skins.

"Where do you sleep?" asked Geoffrey.

"Oh," said Mr Furbelow, "I've got a little cottage near the stables which I bought for my late wife. He didn't change that. I have my things there and I like to keep an eye on them. I do hope you'll be comfortable. Good night."

Before they slept (and in the end they found it was easiest to put the mattresses on the floor – they kept slipping off the chests) Geoffrey said, "How on earth did you pull that off?"

"Oh, I *can* speak Latin. Everybody can at our school. You have to speak it all the time, even at meals, and you get whipped if you make a mistake."

The furs were warm and clean. In that last daze that comes before sleep drowns you, Geoffrey wondered where the weatherman had got to.

10

THE DIARY

Geoffrey couldn't tell what time he woke, but the shadows on the forest trees made it look as if the sun was quite high already. Sally was still fast asleep, muffled in a yellow fur and breathing with contented snorts. He looked out of the window into the hall and saw that the feast was still there, though the dogs had been at it in places, scattering dishes and pulling the whole boar's head on to the floor, where two of them wrenched at opposite ends of it. He felt stupid and sick, which might have been the wine, and very stiff, which must have been yesterday's climbing and running. His clothes were muddy and torn. In one of the chests he found some baggy leggings, with leather thongs to bind them into place, and in another a beautifully soft leather jerkin. There was a belt on the wall, too, carrying a short sword in a bronze scabbard, pierced and patterned with owls and fig leaves. He buckled it round the jerkin and went down into the hall to see if the dogs had left any of the food undefiled.

They were enormous things, very woolly and smelly, big boned, a yellowy-grey colour. Wolfhounds, he decided. Two of them lurched towards him, snarling, but backed away when he drew his sword. He found that they'd only messed up a tiny amount of the hillocks of food spread down the tables, so he filled a tray with fruit and bread and cold chops and looked round for something to drink. The thought of wine or mead or ale made him sick, and after Mr Furbelow's warning about the water he decided it would be safer to boil it, if only he could find a pot to put on the fire. He was afraid the gold and silver vessels might melt, and there didn't seem to be anything else.

In the end he found, hanging between two of the torches, a steel helmet with a chin strap and a pointy top. He used his sword to hollow out a nest in the red embers of the fire, settled the helmet into place and poured water in, spilling enough to cause clouds of steam to join the smoke and waver up towards the hole in the roof. It boiled very fast. He hooked it out by the chin strap and realised that he couldn't put it down because of the point and he had nothing to pour it into, so he held the whole contraption with one hand while he poured the water from one of the big jugs on to the floor and then wine out of a smaller jug into the big one, and at last he could pour his boiled water into the small jug.

When he went to put the blackened helmet back in its place he found a new, shiny one already hanging there. Chilly with fright he carried his tray up to the bedchamber and woke Sally to tell her what had happened.

"*He* must have done it," she said matter of factly.

"Who? Mr Furbelow?"

"Oh, Jeff, don't be tiresome. I mean the 'he' Mr Furbelow keeps talking about, the one who makes all the food and could get rid of the wolves if he felt like it and might put a lot of horses into the stable to keep poor Maddox company. The Nigro man."

"I expect you're right. I just don't want to think about it. I've boiled the water, so it should be all right to drink, but it's still pretty hot. There might be enough left to wash with. You look a right urchin. I found my clobber in the chests, and it mightn't be a bad idea if we looked for something for you. I'm sure Mr Furbelow would like that. He's got himself some pretty elaborate fancy dress. Though I suppose Latin's our best bet. What do you think he means about morphine?"

"I don't know. What is it? Can I have the last chop? You've got three and I've only got two. Do you think he's mad?"

"Morphine's a drug, I think. You give it to soldiers when they're wounded to stop the pain, but I think it's something drug addicts use too, people who take it because they like it and then can't stop. And I don't think he's mad. I mean he isn't just imagining things, or not everything. Somebody must have built this tower and put the forest there – they aren't on the map."

"But I don't think he's *bad* either. I think he's made some sort of mistake and has gone on making it worse and doesn't know how to stop. But I think he might easily be rather touchy. We must be careful what we say to him."

"Yes. And don't push the Latin too hard. Just wait for a natural chance to come up again. Let's see if we can find some clothes for you."

Everything in the chest was really much too big for a ten-year-old girl, but they found a long emerald tabard with bits of red silk appliquéd to it and intricate patterns of gold thread filling the gaps. On Sally it reached to the ground, almost, but when it was pulled in with a big gold belt it looked OK; there weren't any sleeves, so they left her brown arms bare. They found a silver comb in another small chest and did her hair into two pigtails tied with gold ribbon, and when Geoffrey had sponged the mud and sweat off her face she looked quite striking, as if she was about to play the Queen in a charade. There was still no sign of Mr Furbelow so they carried the tray down to the hall and started to explore the rest of the tower.

There were two storeys of rooms in the gallery, all just like theirs, full of chests and furs. The ones in the lower storey were all separate, but the higher ones ran into each other all the way round, with heavy curtains across the doorways, but with nobody in them at all. There was no sound in the whole tower except the crash of a log falling into the fire, followed by a squabble of disturbed hounds. It was very confusing, like a maze. Halfway round they found another ladder going up still further. It led them out on to the roof.

They stood in the open air, still only a third of the way up a dizzy funnel of inward-leaning stone. An open timber staircase climbed spirally up inside this tube of rough-hewn yellow boulders, and finished in a wooden balcony running all the way round inside the parapet. The roof they stood on was a flat cone, with the smoke hole at its point and drainage holes cut into the wall round its perimeter. As they climbed the endless timbers of the stairway Geoffrey noticed that you could still see on them the cutting strokes of a great coarse shaping tool. From the balcony they could see the whole valley, with the ridges of the hills mellow in the morning sunlight and the darker treetops smothering and unshaping everything in between. The children felt oppressed by those million million leaves. The bare upland beyond seemed suddenly a place of escape, if they ever did escape.

Geoffrey leaned over the parapet, his palms chilly with the knowledge of height, to study the courtyard. It was really nothing except the ground enclosed by the outer wall, against which leaned a higgledy-piggledy line of pitched roofs, tiled with stone and slate. They looked very scrappy from up here, like the potting sheds and timber stores and huts where mowers are kept which you can usually find behind privet hedges in the concealed nooks of a big garden. They seemed just to have grown there. In one place this ill-planned mess gave way to a neat modern building, set askew to the wall, finished in whitewashed stucco, with proper sash windows and steep slate steps leading up to a yellow front door. While they were staring at it the door opened and Mr Furbelow came out carrying a tray. The old man stood for a moment, blinking in the keen sunlight like a roosting bird disturbed by a torch beam, and then tittupped down the steps with an easy little run that showed he'd done it a thousand times before.

"He's going to come a cropper one of these days," said Geoffrey.

"What's that he's carrying?" asked Sally.

She wasn't tall enough to see over the parapet, so she'd wriggled herself up on to the warm gold stone and was lying on it face down, craning over the dizzy edge. Geoffrey grabbed angrily at her belt.

"Don't be a nit, Sal. There's nothing to hold on to."

"There's no reason to fall off either. What *has* he got?"

It was a white tray, with a white cloth on it covering some lumpy shapes. Geoffrey felt that he ought to know what it meant; it didn't seem to belong to this world of battlements and saffron-soaked chicken and wolfhounds scratching and snarling round a central fire. Suddenly he saw a picture, sucked out of forgotten times but very clear, of his mother in bed in a room full of medicine smells and smells of floor polish, with a nurse walking past carrying a tray like Mr Furbelow's.

"It's a hospital tray," he said.

"D'you think he's going to see *him*. He did say that about morphine."

They watched Mr Furbelow move across the cobbles to what Geoffrey had decided was a second well, with a heavy, roped windlass above it. Here the old man put the tray down and started to crank the handle. He turned it for ages, so that it seemed as if the well must be enormously deeper than that from which they'd watered Maddox.

"Oh look, Jeff. The stone's moved. I can just see the edge of it from here. It's enormous."

Geoffrey moved along the parapet and saw what she meant. The side of a thick flagstone, a huge one, had been heaved out of the ground and a pitch-black opening showed beneath. The handle winding hadn't been because the well was deep, but because the windlass had to be highly geared to allow Mr Furbelow to shift a stone that weight. At last he stopped cranking, picked up the tray and felt his way into the hole. From the jerky way his body moved as he disappeared they could see he was going down steps.

"Quick, Sal, now's our chance to find something out."

They bolted down the long spiral of steps, through the trap in the roof, down the ladders and into the hall where the hounds lounged. The big doors were barred from the outside; Geoffrey shoved and tugged, but they moved as little as a rooted yew.

The children climbed back to the parapet and waited in the generous sun. They were feeling hungry again before Mr Furbelow came out.

While he was cranking the flagstone back into place Geoffrey said, "I've had a thought – we don't want him to think we've been spying on him. Let's try and find a window downstairs from which we can see him going back to his house but can't see the windlass. If I leave my handkerchief on the balcony we'll be able to keep our bearings when we get down."

It wasn't easy, even so, and they got it wrong first time. Then they found a suite of rooms with the tiny square windows tunnelled through the masonry, from one of which they could see the white cottage. The ratchet of the windlass was still clacking monotonously.

"We can shout, I suppose," said Geoffrey, "but he'll never see us in here. We might try poking a cloth out on a stick."

"I could wriggle along and poke my head out. Lift me up."

"Don't get stuck. It isn't worth it."

She squirmed into the opening, working herself along with toes and elbows. When she stopped Geoffrey could only just reach her feet. The folds of the tabard completely filled the square, blotting out the sunlight and the noise of the ratchet. He was mad to let her go in without taking it off – it would ruck up if she came back and make it twice as hard for her to get out if she stuck.

"Mr Furbeloo-ow! Mr Furbeloo-ow! Please can you come and let us out?"

Faintly Geoffrey heard an answering shout, and Sally began to wriggle back. He reached into the hole and pulled at the hem of the tabard so that it couldn't bundle itself up and cork her in. She slid to the floor grinning.

"He nearly dropped the tray. He's gone into the house but he says he'll be coming in a minute. Have I messed myself up?"

"Not too bad. Your cheek's dirty. I'll go and get some water."

"Use lick. I don't mind."

They went down and waited by the big doors. At last there was a squeaking and rattling outside, and when Geoffrey shoved, the door groaned slowly open. Mr Furbelow looked tired, but was gushingly apologetic.

"My dear young things, I am so sorry. I am in the habit of shutting the dogs in, you see, and to tell the truth I had completely forgotten your presence here. On the days when I have to visit him I find it hard to think of anything else. I do apologise. And goodness, it must be nearly lunch time. I hope he left some food for your breakfast. Shall we eat at once?"

"Please, Mr Furbelow," said Sally, "may I go and see if Maddox is all right? And could I let him out into the courtyard for a bit?"

"Of course, my dear, of course. How well that attire suits you, like a little Maid Marian. You two go and look after your pony, and then come and join me for a bite of food."

Maddox was in a bitter temper, snarling at Geoffrey and trying to work him into a corner where he could be properly bitten. Sally pretended not to notice, scratched him between the ears, found another cube of horse-bait and led him out into the courtyard, where he yawned at the magic tower, sneered at the delicious sunlight and began to scratch his sagging belly with a hind hoof. Then he noticed some green grass growing between cobbles and cheered up. They left him systematically weeding the whole paved area and walked into the cavern of the tower.

Mr Furbelow was talking baby talk with a funny Welsh lilt to one of the wolfhounds; the uncouth monster lay on its back, legs waggling in an ecstasy of adoration, while he rubbed its chest with his foot.

"Aren't you afraid of them?" said Geoffrey. "They frightened me stiff this morning when I came down to get some food."

"Oh dear me, no, I'm not afraid. I love dogs, though I really wanted corgis but I couldn't make him understand. But in any case he wouldn't let me be hurt – he said so. If you tried to hit me on the head or your pony tried to kick me he'd prevent it."

"Would he stop you hurting yourself – by accident?"

"I don't know. I hadn't thought of that. But I don't think it's likely to happen. Shall we have a go at this side of beef. They seemed to prefer it rather high, I'm afraid, but sometimes you can eat it. Oh dear. I think we won't risk it. You take that end, Geoffrey, and I'll take this, and we'll drag it to the fire for the dogs. Don't try to do it all yourself, it's much too heavy. Oh dear, what it is to be young and strong. I must ask you to give me a hand with one or two things this afternoon, too trivial to bother him about. Now, let's see."

He walked down the long table sniffing suspiciously at the mighty slabs of meat, muttering and clucking and shaking his head, and eventually settled for a peacock with all its tail feathers in place. The dark meat was chewy but pleasant, but the stuffing was disgusting. Most of the strawberries had gone mouldy overnight, but there were some delicious apricots. Mr Furbelow insisted that they must peel these, as they had probably been ripened on dungheaps.

"Did he make all this food out of nothing?" asked Geoffrey. "Or does it come from somewhere? I boiled some water in a helmet this morning and when I'd finished there was another helmet on the wall. Did he make this tower all at once, like that, or did it take him days and days?"

"Oh dear, I don't know how he does it. The tower came in a night, and he took my cottage away but I made him get it back because it had the drugs in it. I think this is all a copy of something; bits of it look so used and all those clothes seem to belong to real people. I think it's the same with the food. Sometimes these big pastry things look as if they'd been made for a special occasion. I often think they're not even copies – they're the real things and he's just moved them about in time."

"Then why aren't there any people?" said Sally.

"Oh dear, it's difficult, isn't it? I've asked him that, before I lost him completely, and he said something about 'natura'. I think he meant it was wrong somehow to do to people what he's done to the tower and the food – it's against nature. I suppose that's why he doesn't stop the food going bad, too, but he is so difficult now, and he gets so impatient when I have to look things up in the dictionary, and it's all so different from everything I meant."

"Would you like me to come and help?" said Sally. "I could do the Latin if you'd tell me what to say."

The old chemist, who'd been practically snivelling with misery at the end of his last speech, opened his mouth to say "no", but instead he made a funny sucking noise, and sat for several seconds with his mouth wide open, staring at her. He looked as if he were going to cry, but instead he shook his head and sighed.

"Too late, too late. If you'd come four years ago, perhaps... But you cannot get through to him now and even if you could the withdrawal..."

The old, despairing voice dwindled into mumblings.

"You said that yesterday," said Geoffrey. "What does it mean?"

"Ah, well, you see... but I don't know if it's suitable... what your parents... oh, you haven't any. I do apologise... oh dear, this will never do..."

More silence. Then Mr Furbelow squared his shoulders and spoke in a changed, dry voice, like a teacher rattling through a boring lesson.

"Certain drugs are what is called habit-forming. This does not just mean that the people who take them like them and want to go on taking them but that their whole body comes to like them too, so much so that every muscle and cell seems to scream if the drugs are withdrawn. Hence the phrase 'withdrawal symptom'.

The disappointed addict may become both mad and violent, and with a creature of such power as his..."

The voice returned to its normal dazed lilt.

"I speak from hearsay, and what I have read, of course. I have never attempted to take drugs myself. The Pharmaceutical Society has very strong views, and so did my late wife... oh dear, I feel I have been very unwise, but my intentions were for the best, they really were, and now I cannot stop. It would be too dangerous, I know it would, particularly if he didn't realise what was happening."

"Couldn't I try to explain to him?" said Sally.

"Oh dear, I suppose we ought to try. I must confess I don't want to, but it may be the only chance, the last chance... Ah, well..."

He sniffed several times and stared into his goblet. Then he drained it and stood up.

"We must go now," he said. "He will be at his best, about now, content with what I have given him and not yet lost in his dreams. He might even have a lucid interval, but his reactions are not like other people's. Come, let us get it over with. Geoffrey, you can turn that filthy crank for me, but I will go down alone with Sally. You must promise not to follow us and come nosing down. I know how inquiring young folks are. I put you on your honour."

"I promise," said Geoffrey. They followed Mr Furbelow out of the hall.

The windlass was harder work than he'd supposed. There was a lot of friction in the wooden cogs and axles, and he wound on and on, surprised at the willpower that enabled Mr Furbelow to drive his doddering body to work the contraption. At last the stone, a great tilted flap of paving, jarred against a crossbeam, and Geoffrey could see coarse steps leading into darkness.

"They're rather steep," said Mr Furbelow. "I'll show you the way."

Sally followed him down.

At first Geoffrey mooned about the area round the windlass, but soon Maddox clumped up, snarling, and drove him off. The pony seemed to know where Sally was, and even tried putting a foot on the top step, but thought better of it and stood staring down into the burrow like a cat nosing at a mousehole or a lover gazing at the window of his beloved. Geoffrey left him to it.

The second time he passed the white cottage he decided to explore. He could see Maddox from the steps, still standing like a stuffed animal in a museum. Any movement from the pony would be a warning that someone was coming out. The yellow door was ajar. The hall was a clutter of dumped objects, with just room to walk between them. There was that funny smell of damp and dirt that you sometimes find in houses where nobody does any proper cleaning. Upstairs were two rooms, one a dusty boxroom and the other a pretty, pink room with two beds in it. Downstairs was a kitchen with a Calor gas cooker, but it didn't look as if it had been used for ages; a back door led out to the angle between the outer wall of the tower and the house. Opposite the kitchen, across the hall, was the room Geoffrey wanted.

This was where Mr Furbelow lived and kept his belongings. There were rows of chemist's bottles on shelves and more chemistry-looking things in cardboard cartons piled along a wall. Most of the books on the shelves were about chemistry and medicine, and there were piles of *Pharmaceutical Journals*. The only furniture in the room was a very ragged sofa with some rugs on it, which looked as though this was where Mr Furbelow usually slept, and a big desk with an upright chair. There was a photograph on the desk, of a smiling, plump, dark-haired woman with her hair in a big bun.

Beside her lay two dictionaries, one Latin-English and the other English-Latin. In the middle of the desk was an account book. The latest entry read:

morph 6 gr: Very restless. Would not talk to me at all, but kept muttering to himself. Shouted 'Quamdiu' several times, and once (I think) 'Regem servavi dum infantem'. I begin to believe his speech is more slurred than it was. Hope this is no bad symptom, but can find nothing in my books. He suddenly was disturbed by something, and almost stood up. Instead he went into a trance, and I heard a tremendous noise of thunder outside. There was a small storm disappearing over the eastern hills when I came out. Nothing like this for months.

Geoffrey glanced out of the window. Maddox was still at his post. The rest of the book was full of short entries, every other day, sometimes just a note of the dose. There was always at least that. On the bookshelf Geoffrey found four similar account books, all full of entries, and next to them a proper diary with the dates printed on each page. The first half of the year was almost empty, except for notes of visits to K's grave, but on the 17th of May there was a longer one.

A most extraordinary thing, which I must record in full. Last spring dear K planted at Llanthony a flowering cherry. _Prunus longipes_ it said on the label. She used often to say, after Doctor H told us the ill news, that she would never see it in flower, but at our last visit before she went into hospital – because of the shop we could only come up at weekends – it was in perfect flower, but deep yellow. This was October, and it was supposed to bear white flowers in late April. We laughed and cried and imagined the nursery had made a mistake. But when I came up here last month – I could not endure to come before – it was in flower again, big white dangling bunches like upside-down powder puffs. Perhaps I ought to have got in touch with some botanical body, but I felt it would be a desecration of dear K's tree. Instead, thinking there might be some peculiarity in the soil, I took samples back to town for analysis. I did the work myself, and either I am mad or it is full of gold!

There were no entries for a week, then a short one:

I have begun to dig at Llanthony. Difficult without disturbing the roots of K's tree. I am tunnelling down and then sideways. I feel compelled to do this.

Next weekend he had dug still further and had taken more samples, which were also rich with gold. The entry after that was longer; Geoffrey read it, glancing out of the window between sentences.

Now I know! But I do not know what to do. I have been digging for the past two weekends, leaving little Gwynnedd to care for the shop on Saturdays. It was not for the gold – I felt I had to do it, just to know. It was hard work for a middle-aged man, but I kept on, and yesterday at noon I struck a smooth, sloping rock. It seemed that I must be at the end of my tunnel, and either give in or dig somewhere else. Then I saw a crack in the rock that seemed too straight to be a fault. I cleared a larger area and uncovered a shaped, rectangular stone. With great difficulty I levered this out. There was a hole behind it, into which I crawled and found myself in a low cavern, full of a dim green light. I thought it must be an ancient burial chamber, for on a slab in the centre there was the body of a very big man, and very hairy. I thought he must be dead, and preserved by some freak which produced the green light too, but when I touched him his flesh was firm and far colder than the coldest ice. It burnt like solid CO_2. But I knew for certain he was alive.

Then I saw that there were letters on the side of the slab. They said HERLINUS SUh. QUI hE TANGIT TURBAT hUNDUh. Latin, I think, but I cannot buy a dictionary until tomorrow. I left, and leaned the stone back into its place.

There was a three-day gap, and then another entry.

I have decided what to do. I cannot leave him and go. I feel sure that I was meant to find him, and that the tree and the gold were signs for me, and me alone. I know that he has enormous powers. I could feel this in the cavern, and that in my hands he could use those powers for good. In what way I do not yet know. Perhaps he might even stop these wicked wars in the Far East, or bring dear K back to me.

The problem is to bind him to me, and I can think of only one way of doing this. If I administer, while he is still asleep, a series of injections of some habit-forming drug (morphine would be simplest), then he will have to do what I say when I wake him, or he will get no more. I fear this does not sound very moral, but I really do intend to try and use him for the good of mankind. Pray heaven that I turn out to be justified.

The Latin, I think, means 'I am Merlin. He who touches me upsets the world'. I have already touched him. I cannot change that.

Phew, thought Geoffrey, things certainly hadn't turned out as Mr Furbelow intended. Fancy expecting to make Merlin his slave! Other way round now, from the look of it. He began to turn on, looking for an account of the wakening, when out of the corner of his eye he saw Maddox move. Geoffrey put the diary back in its place and slipped out through the back door. He ran down a long empty shed full of perches for hawks and climbed through the open window at the far end. From here he was out of sight, and could saunter back towards the windlass, noticing for the first time, as he did so, the flowering cherry that had started all the upheaval.

Mr Furbelow was already winding the slab down into position, and Sally was talking to Maddox, her face as white as a limed wall.

11

THE NECROMANCER

Geoffrey sensed at once that it wouldn't do to ask how the interview had gone. He took over the crank in silence, and lowered the stone. Then Mr Furbelow solicitously led Sally into his cottage and made her lie down on one of the upstairs beds, and he himself settled down for a nap on his sofa. Geoffrey was left to explore, but found nothing of interest, and spent most of the afternoon looking for birds from the tower over the outer gate. He didn't see anything uncommon, but he fancied he heard a wood warbler several times.

They supped early and went to bed when there was still grey light seeping through the outer window. As soon as he was lying down Sally, who had been very quiet all evening, spoke:

"Jeff, you've got to *do* something. He's killing him, really he is. It was all about making a sword this afternoon, but full of words I didn't know. It's awful. He doesn't know what's happening to him, and he's so marvellous, you can feel his mind all strong and beautiful, and Mr Furbelow is killing him. I tried and tried, but he wouldn't hear what I was saying. His Latin's a bit funny, the way he says it, but you soon get used to it. And goodness he's big. Do you remember – no, you won't – there was a dancing bear came to Weymouth once. *It* was beautiful and strong, and it had to do this horrible thing with everyone laughing and jeering and a chain round its neck. He's like that, only worse, much worse. It's horrible. Jeff, please!"

"Oh, Lord, Sal. I'll try and think of something. Did you know he was Merlin?"

"Yes. It said so on the stone where he was lying. How did you?"

He told her about the diary, but before he'd finished she was asleep. He lay on his back with his hand under his head and thought round in circles until he was asleep too. It all depended on Mr Furbelow.

But next morning Mr Furbelow had changed. He was still polite and kind, but when they tried to talk about Merlin he said that that was his concern; and at lunch he told them that he would prefer them to leave next day. They were upsetting things, he said. They needn't bother about the wolves, because they could give them the rest of the feast tonight and wolves sleep for twenty-four hours after a full meal. That was settled then, wasn't it? He'd be sorry to see them go, but really it was for the best.

In the afternoon, for an experiment, Sally managed to manoeuvre Maddox into a position where he could take a good kick at Mr Furbelow as the old man snoozed in a ramshackle deck chair in front of the house. The pony shaped happily for the kick, but suddenly danced away as if it had been stung and would not go near the place again. So that was no good. Nor, presumably, would be hitting him on the head with something, even if Geoffrey had managed to bring himself to do it. Geoffrey trudged round and round the tower, frowning. Mr Furbelow would hear the windlass clack if they tried to raise the stone when he was asleep, and anyway it would be no use seeing Merlin if Mr Furbelow was going to continue pumping drugs into him afterwards.

He came around the tower for the twentieth time, and saw Mr Furbelow, awake now, do his funny skitter down the steps. If only he would fall on them he might break a leg. They really were hideously dangerous, and that was the only hope. He must be made to fall.

The three of them dined together very friendlily. Most of the meat was high by now, but they found a leg of sweet, thymy mutton. Then, in the dusk, Mr Furbelow showed them some funny long wheelbarrows without any sides in one of the sheds, and they wheeled load after load of bad meat to the outer tower and threw it through the wicket gate. The wolves were already there by the time they brought the second load, snarling and tugging at the big joints. As they watched, more and more of the long shadowy bodies flitted out of the blackness under the trees. There were several mother-wolves with cubs which waited, eyes green in the half-light, until their mother dragged a big hunk for them and they could begin a snarling match of their own.

When the last of the meat had been ferried away from the tables Mr Furbelow barred the children into the tower. Two hours later Geoffrey stood at the parapet in his gold robe and thought of rain.

All day the island had slumbered in the sun. It was

warm, warm, and above it the warmed air rose, sucking in the winds off the western ocean, disturbed winds heavy with wetness, only just holding their moisture over the smooth, tepid sea. And now meeting the land, already cool with night, cooler now, cooler still, and the hills reforming the clouds, jostling them together, piling them up, squeezing them till the released rain hissed into the hills' sere grasses. Now trees drip, leaves glisten in faint light, forgotten gullies tinkle. Rain, swathed, drumming...

Sally, wrapped in drenched furs, led him down the long stairs to shelter. He squatted in a corner, deliberately uncomfortable, so that he woke every half hour. When it was still dark he put his soaking robe on over a dry jerkin and went up to the parapet again. The last rain had gone, and starlight glistened in every puddle and drip. It was very cold already. He thought of frost.

Still air chilling the hills. Evaporation chilling the ground. The trees ceasing their breathing. An icy influence from the stars. Rivers of cold air flowing down, weaving between the trunks, coming here to make a deep pool of cold, crisping the grass. Cat-ice now in crackles on the puddles, white-edged round hoofprints, ice glazing cobbles and stones in a shiny film. A deep, hard frost, making earth ring like iron. Deep, hard, deep...

This time he was woken from the weather-trance by the violent shivering of his own body. The robe was starched rigid with ice, and his legs so numb with cold and standing that he couldn't feel his feet. He had to clutch the guardrail all the way down to the roof, and even so he nearly fell twice on the ice-crusted steps. He warmed himself by the never-dying fire in the hall, watched by yawning hounds, and then went up to the gallery. As he snuggled into his furs he was struck by a nasty snag in his plans. The doors would still be barred, but if all went right Mr Furbelow wouldn't be able to open them. Sulkily he crawled out of the warmth and rootled through several chambers for belts. Ten ought to be enough. He hacked the buckles off and tied the straps into a single length with a loop at the end. And then sleep.

It was a bright day when he woke. Sally was shaking his shoulder.

"OK, OK, I'm awake. Has Mr Furbelow come out yet?"

"I didn't look. I've brought some fruit and bread up for breakfast."

"Hang on. I'll just go and see what's up."

He ran down the stairs, carrying his leather rope. The hounds were used to him by now. Up the third ladder, which led to the suite overlooking the cottage. He peered through the small, square opening. Mr Furbelow had already come out, and was lying in an awkward mess at the bottom of the icy steps. He didn't move.

"Sal!" shouted Geoffrey, realising in sweaty panic that perhaps the kind old man was dead and he'd murdered him, "Sal!"

She came into the chamber, flushed from running up the ladder.

"Look, Sal, Mr Furbelow's slipped and fallen on the steps. You've got to crawl out backwards with this loop round your foot. Don't lose it. Then when you're over the edge you can stand on the loop and hold on to the straps and I'll let you down; then you can run round and open the door and we can go and see if he's all right."

"I'll take my dress off. Don't worry, Jeff, I'm sure he's all right. Anyway it was the only thing you could have done. You'll have to lift me up."

It was much more awkward getting her in backwards, and the loop wouldn't stay on her foot. But then she was slithering down the tunnel, scrabbling at the edge, and then out of sight. The knots snagged on the far sill, so that he had to lower her in a series of jerks. When he was holding the last belt the whole contraption went slack and he heard her calling that she was down. He ran to the doors.

"Jeff, you'll have to wait. I can't reach the bar. I'm going to fetch Maddox."

Silence. A long wait. The hounds scratched and the fire, which he'd never seen fed, hissed sappily. Outside a pigeon cooed its boring June coo. Then the clop of hooves.

"Stop there, Maddox. Good old boy. No, stand still while I climb up. That's it. Golly, it's heavy. I don't think..."

A scratching noise and a clunk. Geoffrey heaved at the door and it swung open.

Mr Furbelow was lying on one side, with his leg bent back under him. He was breathing snortily, with his mouth open. Geoffrey ran into the cottage, nearly slipping on the icy steps himself, and brought out the sofa cushions. They eased him on to these and straightened him out on his back. His left leg seemed to be broken somewhere above the knee. Geoffrey decided he'd better try and set it while the old man was still unconscious. Trying to remember everything that Uncle Jacob had shown him ("Decide slowly, laddie, and do it quickly and firmly. No room for squeamishness in a sick bay") he felt the bones into position. There was one place where they seemed right. Then he used his sword to lever the back off one of the kitchen chairs, bandaged the leg with torn strips of pillowcase from the bedroom, and lashed the uprights of the chair-back down the leg with the knotted belts. It was very tiresome to do without unsettling the join, even with the leg propped on cushions, and when he'd finished it looked horribly clumsy, but he felt as if it ought to hold the break firm for a bit. Sally went into the hall to fetch a jug of wine, but before she was back the old man blinked and groaned.

"Morphine," he muttered. "Top right-hand drawer of my desk. Hypodermic syringe, bottle of spirit there too. Don't touch anything else."

There was a box of morphine ampoules, three hypodermic syringes and what Geoffrey took to be the spirit bottle.

"Watch carefully," said Mr Furbelow. He took the things on to his chest, dipped the point of the needle into the spirit and then prodded through the rubber at the end of the ampoule, withdrawing the plunger to suck the liquid out. Then he tilted it up, pressed the plunger until a drop showed at the point of the needle, and pushed the point into a vein on the inside of his left arm, squeezing the morphine slowly into his bloodstream. You could see the pain screaming from his eyes. Golly, thought Geoffrey, he's a brave old man and I've done a wicked thing. He decided to tell him the truth, but Mr Furbelow seemed to have fainted again. They watched him for five minutes. Then he spoke, not opening his eyes.

"That's better. Have you contrived to do anything about my leg?"

"Yes, Mr Furbelow. I hope I've done the right thing. I tried to set it, and it felt as if it was together properly, and then I put splints on it. I *am* sorry. It must hurt frightfully."

"What had we best do about *him*?" said Mr Furbelow.

"If you'll tell me what to do, I'll try and do it properly. Sally can talk to him if necessary. If it's the best we can manage he'll have to put up with it."

"He will not like the change, I fear. He is the most conservative of creatures."

"Would you like us to try and carry you into your house? It won't be very easy, but I expect I could rig something up."

"Let us leave that, for the moment. Perhaps he will be so angry that he will destroy us all, or perhaps he will mend my leg. In either case the effort will have been pointless. Now, Geoffrey, do you remember what I did with the syringe? It is most important to squeeze a drop out with the point upwards, so that you do not inject any air into the bloodstream."

"I think I can cope."

"Then I suggest you get it over. You give him three ampoules in each arm, and he likes to take his time about it. And some of the rubber has begun to perish, so that it is best to take a few spares. I usually carry everything on the tray which you'll find beside the bookshelf in my study."

Geoffrey went in and got the equipment together. Mr Furbelow said nothing as they passed him on the way out. The cranking seemed to take half an hour, but at last the stone gave the dull thud which meant it was high enough.

"I'll go first," said Sally. "It's not really as dark as it looks – he makes a sort of light at the bottom. You've got to feel each step with your foot because they're all different. Are you going to give him the drug?"

"Not if I can help it."

They felt their way down the coarse stone. The steps did not feel like shaped work at all – more like flattened boulders from a river bed, pitted with the endless rubbing of water and patterned with fossil bones. There were thirty-three of them. At the bottom a passage led away through rock towards a faint green light. It was eleven paces down the passage and into a long, low chamber whose rock walls sloped inwards like the roof of an attic. The air in the chamber smelt sweet and wild and wrong, like rotting crab apples. Merlin was waiting for them.

He lay on his side, with his head resting on the crook of his arm, staring up the passage. Perhaps he had been aroused to expect them by the clack of the ratchet. He wore a long, dark robe. Colours were difficult in the strange light, but his beard seemed black and his face the colour of rusted iron. His eyes were so deep in the huge head that they looked like the empty sockets of a skull until you moved across their beam and saw the green glow reflected from the lens, like the reflection of sky at the bottom of a well. The light seemed to come from nowhere. It was just there, impregnating the sick, sweet atmosphere.

He gave no sign, made no movement, as Sally crossed his line of vision, but his head followed Geoffrey into the room – no, not Geoffrey, the white tray. Geoffrey found he was gripping the tray so hard that the tin rim hurt his palms. With a struggle, like a man turning into a gale at a street corner, he turned away from Merlin and put the tray on the paving behind him. When he turned back Merlin had moved, rearing up on to his elbow. He was a giant. The black hair streamed down in a wild mane behind him. His eyes were alive now, and the chamber was throbbing with a noiseless hum, like the hum of a big ship's engines which you cannot hear with your ears but sings up from the deck through your feet, through your shoulder when you lean against a stanchion, and through your whole body as you lie in your bunk waiting for sleep. His lips moved.

"Ubi servus meus?"

The voice was a grey scrape, like shingle retreating under the suck of a wave. Sally answered in a whisper.

"Magister Furbelow crurem fregit."

Merlin did not look at her. The green glaze of his

eyes clanged into Geoffrey's skull, drowning his will in a welter of dithering vibrations. A vast forearm slid towards him, revealing on its inner surface flesh pocked with a thousand needle-pricks. The lips moved again. "Da mihi cibum meum."

Mastered, helpless, Geoffrey went through the ritual of disinfection and filling which Mr Furbelow had shown him. He held the needle-point upwards and squeezed until a round drop shone green in the green light – a point, a focus, a thing to concentrate on. He seized it with his remaining mind.

"Tell him it's poison," he gasped. Sally answered with a quick babble.

"Venenum est, domine. Venenum. Venenum mentis. *Tute* servus es, domine. Servus veneni. Indignum est nominis tui. Deliras ob venenum. Crede mihi, crede. Indignum est…"

The maned head swung round towards Sally, and Geoffrey found he could move too. She was saying the same words over and over again, not whispering any more but shouting with urgency, trying to ram her message through six years of poisoned stupor. Her cheeks were runnelled with tears – she was thinking of the dancing bear. She shouted on and on the same words, "venenum mentis... indignum... crede mihi..." until she was gasping between each syllable and her voice cracked with pain. Merlin stared at her like an entomologist considering an insect, and at last sighed. Sally stopped shouting.

He turned to Geoffrey and held out his slab of arm again.

"Da," he said.

Dim, fuzzy, drowned in failure, Geoffrey lifted the hypodermic. Then he realised the gesture was somehow different: it was not the arm but the hand which was reaching forward. The palm was covered with fine black hairs. He put the hypodermic into it and the fingers closed. Merlin heaved his body again and was now sitting on the slab, his legs dangling, his head bowed so as not to touch the roof. He must have been nearly eight foot tall. He turned the hypodermic over and over in his hands, intent, withdrawn, like an ape examining a twig. Suddenly he put the two outer fingers of his right hand over it and the middle and ring fingers until it and squeezed. The glass splintered, the metal buckled, the morphine ran down his robe.

"Abite," he said. "Gratias ago."

"Sal, tell him about the withdrawal symptoms. Tell

him that there are two more hypodermics and some more morphine if he wants to try and give it up slowly."

Sally embarked on a long, urgent whisper. Merlin stared at her as she spoke and at last shook his head.

"Intellexi," he said. "Perdurabo, deo volente."

He settled back on to the implacable stone. The green light dimmed. Geoffrey picked up the tray. They left.

Geoffrey stopped on the stairs.

"What did you say to him?" he asked.

"I told him it was poison, poison of the mind. I told him he was its slave – he'd called Mr Furbelow his slave before. I told him that it was – oh, there isn't an English word for indignum – shameful, unworthy, not honourable – they all sound so soppy. I told him the poison was making him mad. Then he said thank you and told us to go away. Then I told him about the withdrawal, and he said he'd – he'd – stick it out, I suppose."

"But he said thank you," said Geoffrey.

"Yes," said Sally.

8

WITHDRAWAL

It felt as if it should be late afternoon as they came up the steps, but it was still morning, the sun just sucking up the last of the melted ice from the night before. Not knowing whether it was the right thing to do, he lowered the slab over the tunnel and carried the tray towards the cottage.

Mr Furbelow had his eyes open. He too had been roused by the clack of the ratchet and was waiting for them.

"Did he miss me?" he said.

"Yes," said Geoffrey. "He noticed at once."

"Ah," said Mr Furbelow. Silence. "And he took it from you all right?"

"I hope you won't be cross," said Sally, "but we persuaded him to try and give it up."

"You did what?"

"We told him it was poison."

Mr Furbelow shut his eyes and sighed. He looked as frail as a last year's leaf.

"Do you want us to carry you into your house?" said Geoffrey.

"No thank you. I am better here."

"Then we must try and build you some sort of shelter."

There were a lot of curious tools in one of the sheds, great adzes and odd-shaped choppers. There were blunt and clumsy saws, too, and another shed was a well-stocked timber-store. Geoffrey prized out four cobbles at the corners of Mr Furbelow's bed with his sword – they were pigs to move, each packed tight against its neighbours and jammed by century-hardened dirt. He loosened the exposed ground and walloped four pointed uprights into position, staying them with what he took to be bowstrings, which he tied to knives jammed between cobbles further out. He nailed a framework of lighter timbers on to the uprights, and fastened to this the most waterproof-looking of the furs Sally had brought out from the tower. The whole contraption took him about six hours to build, so, what with stopping for lunch (stale bread and cheese, apricots and souring wine) and ministering to Mr Furbelow's needs (the old man was quiet and dignified now, but gave himself another shot of morphine towards evening) it was drawing on to dusk by the time he had finished. Venus glimmered in a pale wash of sky above the western hill-line before the first symptom occurred.

All the hounds in the tower began howling together, a crazy, terrifying yammer, interrupted by choruses of hoarse barking. A moment's silence, and they spilt into the courtyard, howling again, dashing to and fro under the tower wall, biting fiercely at each other with frothing mouths until the yellow fur was streaked with dirty red blood. Geoffrey drew his sword and told Sally to run to the house if they came any nearer, but the madness stopped with a couple of coughs, like a fading engine, and the dogs crept away to lick their wounds and whimper under the eaves of the timber store.

The evening deepened and the air chilled. Geoffrey went to spread the lightest pelt over Mr Furbelow and to let down the sheltering flaps at the side of his bed. One of the guy ropes had gone slack, and when he tried to tauten it he found that the crack into which he had driven its knife was now half an inch wide. The ground had moved.

"Sal, I think you'd better get Maddox out into the open. Anything might happen tonight. I'll look for more rugs and food, if there's any left."

He jammed the knife into another crack and went into the tower. One of the big doors was off its hinges. Inside all the flambeaux were smoking, and the fire too was sending up a heavy grey column which didn't seem to be finding its way out of the hole in the roof. The huge room was full of choking haze, and a voice was shrieking from the upper gallery: "Mordred. Mordred. Mordred." It went on and on. One of the long tables had been overturned, leaving a mess of fruit and bread and dishes spilt across the floor, but on the other he found a bowl of tiny apples and some untouched loaves. He carried them out to the cottage steps, where Sally sat wrapped in a white fur.

"Get as much wood as you can out of the timber store," he said. "We'd better have a fire. I'll find something to protect Mr Furbelow's leg in case that contraption collapses. It sounds as though there's people in there now, Sal, but I can't see anyone."

"I don't think he'd hurt us on purpose," said Sally.

This time the smoke in the tower was worse. The voice had stopped but there was a clashing and tinkling on the far side of the hall, interspersed with hoarse gruntings. He couldn't see what was happening because of the smoke, but suddenly grasped that this must be the noise people make when they are fighting with shield and sword. He picked up a bench and began to carry it out, but before he reached the door there came a burst of wild yelling behind him and the running of feet. Something struck him on his left shoulder, he staggered and then something much solider caught him on the hip and threw him sideways across the bench he was carrying in a clumsy somersault. He crouched there as the feet thudded past, but saw nothing. When they had gone the voice began shrieking again: "Mordred. Mordred. Mordred." It was lower in tone now, but still the same woman's voice, hoarse and murderous. He picked up his bench and limped away, the pain where the thing had hit him nagging at his hip. Sally had gathered a useful pile of timber.

"We'll want small stuff to start with," said Geoffrey, "and straw out of the stables. Did you see anyone come out of the tower? Somebody knocked me over but it's so full of smoke that I couldn't see what was happening."

"I saw Maddox shying and neighing, and then he went off and made friends with the dogs, but I didn't see anything else. How are you going to light the fire, Jeff?"

"If you'll get straw and kindling, I'll get a burning log out of the hall."

"Do be careful."

"OK. But I don't think being careful is going to make much difference."

The voice had stopped again and there was no noise of fighting. The smoke was thick as the thickest fog. Geoffrey crouched under it and scuttled across the paving until he could see the glow of the fire. Before he reached it he realised there was something in the way, and stopped. It looked like two new pillars, supporting a heavy, shadowy thing. At the same moment as he realised that the pillars had feet, the thing became the back of an armed man, motionless, squat, brooding into the fire. His armour was leather with strips of thick bronze sewn on to it. A tangle of yellow-grey hair flowed over the shoulders from under the horned helmet.

Geoffrey crept away beneath the shelter of the

smoke. When he reached the wall he found a tall stool which he stood on to take one of the flambeaux out of its iron bracket. He decided not to go back into the tower again.

The flame of the straw flared into brightness and died down almost at once, but some of the kindling caught and with careful nursing they made a proper fire, leaning billets of timber into a wigwam round the crackling orange heart. As soon as it was really going the hounds slouched over and arranged themselves in a sprawling circle, scratching, yawning and licking the blood off their coats. Maddox followed and stood in the half-light on the edge of the circle, thinking obscure horse thoughts. Geoffrey placed the bench at right-angles across Mr Furbelow's sleeping form and stayed it firm, to be a second line of defence if the shelter fell. He went into the cottage and brought out the rest of the blankets and the drawer of medicine, which he put into the shelter. Nothing noticeable happened for half an hour, while Sally and he sat on the steps and ate bread and apples.

Then came the storm. The stars which had been blazing down hard-edged as diamonds vanished from horizon to horizon. The sky groaned. Bale-fires pranced along the parapet and flickered down the edges of the tower. A few drops of rain fell, warm as blood, and then the valley cracked with lightning. Geoffrey could see that the dogs were howling again, but he couldn't hear them through the grinding bellows of thunder. There was no darkness. All down the valley the black cloud-roof stood on jigging legs of light, blue-white, visible through closed eyelids. The shed next to the stables caught fire and burnt with orange flames and black, oily smoke. Maddox picked his way between the dogs and nuzzled under Sally's fur, shivering convulsively. The world drowned in noise.

When the storm finished he thought he was deaf. His head was full of a strange wailing, which he decided must be the effect of ruined eardrums. But then a log on the fire tilted sideways and he heard it fall – the wailing was outside, coming from the sky, swooping in great curves around the tower. As it crossed the now blazing stables he thought he saw a darker blackness in the night, bigger than a bird, but wasn't sure. The wailing rose to a tearing squeal and floated away westwards.

Then, he afterwards realised, the disturbances invaded his own mind. At the time it seemed like more portents crowding in round him. A new tower sprouted to the north, with people moving about at the top of it, carrying lanterns. A dark beast, toad shaped, big as a barn, heaved itself out of the forest and scrabbled at the stonework. Uncle Jacob stalked across the cobbles, cracking his thumbs in a shower of sparks; he looked angry, did not speak, and walked on into the dark. The whole landscape started to drift, to float away after the wailing noise, faster and faster, with a whirling, bucking motion, sucked on a roaring current of time which toppled over the edge of reality. They were falling, falling...

The rest, for a while, was dreams, meaningless; shapeless, a dark chaos.

When he woke up it was still dark. The clouds had gone, the moon was well down in the sky, a few patches of embers showed where the stables and the sheds beyond them had been, and the earth was heaving in sudden stiff jerks and spasms. Tiles were clattering off the sheds all round the courtyard, and from the forest came the groaning of toppled trees. The steps on which they were sitting had tilted sideways. Sally lay across him with her head in his lap.

"Wake up, Sal. Wake up and be ready to run. I think the tower might fall."

"Oh, Jeff, I'm frightened."

"So'm I. If it falls straight at us we're done for, but if it looks like going a bit to one side we must run the other way. Don't try to hide in any of the buildings – they might cave in too. I hope Mr Furbelow will be all right."

You couldn't prepare for the spasms, because they weren't rhythmical, just shuddering jars from any direction, often with a deep booming noise underground. Geoffrey looked round to see how the cottage was taking it, and saw in the moonlight a black ragged crack, inches wide, running up the stucco beside the door. They fell over twice as they moved away (it was like trying to stand in a bus without holding on and without looking where it's going). They had to be careful, too, where they put their feet, because of the way the gaps between the cobbles widened and snapped together. They found a patch of flagstones, which seemed safer, and sat back to back, looking up to where the dark wedge of the tower blanked out a huge slice of stars.

They waited for it to fall. It came down quite slowly.

First there were three grunting spasms, all together, and a section of the outer wall over to their right fell with a gravelly roar into the ditch, taking the timber store with it. Then they saw the ground in that direction humping itself up into a wave which came grinding across the courtyard, six feet high, throwing off a spume of cobbles in the moonlight. They stood up. Sally turned to run.

"Face it, Sal. Try and ride over it when it comes. Hold my hand. Run *up*."

The shock wave reached the paved area, tilting the stones over like the leaves of a book being flipped through. Geoffrey ran forward, dragging Sally with him, climbing and scrambling. Sally fell and he leant forwards, heaving at her arm. The stone he was standing on tilted suddenly the other way, breaking his grip and shooting him up on to the crest of the wave and down the other side. A stone fell painfully across his leg, pinning him by the ankle, and then Sally came floundering on top of him.

"Are you all right, Jeff?"

"Yes. Oh look!"

He pointed. The wave was past the tower now, but the tower was falling. First a big triangle of masonry slid out on the far side, broad at the top and narrow at the bottom, like wallpaper peeled downwards off a wall.

The boulders slid, coughing and roaring, down in a continuous avalanche that spilled away from the base right out to the windlass and flagstone over Merlin's chamber. Something deep underground must have given way, for the tower continued to tilt in that direction, slow as the minute-hand of a clock it seemed, but spilling more small avalanches from the ruined lip. It tilted, still almost whole, until it looked as though it could not possibly stand at that angle. Then the flaw below the foundation gave way with a final shudder; the severe curve of the outline crumpled; it was falling in hundreds of colossal fragments; there was one last roar and the tremor of booming hammer-blows jarring the ground beneath them; dust smoked up in a huge pillar, higher than the tower had been, a wavering ghost of the solid stone; silence.

The long hill of rubble, immovable thousands of tons, lay directly over the place where Merlin was buried.

13

TIDYING UP

That was the last upheaval. Soon there was a faint staining of dawn light over the eastern horizon. The courtyard was a wilderness of tumbled stones and half the outer wall was down. Two of the dogs were dead and a third was whining miserably, its leg trapped between cobbles. Maddox stood with his back to the worst of the wreckage, as if to make clear that anything that had happened wasn't his fault. At first Geoffrey, after he'd levered the flagstone away, had thought that his own ankle was broken, but he found he could just stand on it and hobbled over to see what had become of Mr Furbelow. The shelter had collapsed, but the bench had fallen sideways across a protruding mound of cobbles and was still protecting the damaged leg. When Geoffrey cleared the furs and timber away he found the old man staring placidly upwards.

"Would you like some more morphine, sir?"

"No, thank you. Aspirin will be adequate now. There is some on the second shelf behind my desk. What has happened?"

"The tower fell down."

"Ah."

There was a long pause before he spoke again.

"I thought it was beautiful. Strange that we are the only three who ever saw it."

Geoffrey fetched the aspirin and took some himself. Then he tried to free the hound with the trapped leg, but it slashed with its teeth whenever he came close. In the end he threw a fur over its head and twisted the corners, making a sort of tough sack which Sally held tight while he unwedged the stones. They'd been loosened by the earthquake and gave easily. The dog limped away. The children lay down in piles of furs and slept.

They were woken by sunlight and hunger. Geoffrey's leg was very sore, so he took more aspirin and sat while Sally fetched bread and apples; there wasn't much left when they'd finished breakfast.

It was only then that Geoffrey noticed what had happened to the rockpile made by the ruins of the tower. It had contracted into a single solid ridge of unhewn rock, like the cliffs on the higher ground; small stonecrops and grasses already grew from its crannies. Merlin must still be alive, then, deep underground, and had drawn the whole ruin of his tower over him to keep him safe from any future Furbelows. Geoffrey tried to picture him, asleep in the greenish light, cold as solid carbon dioxide, waiting, waiting... He spoke his thought aloud.

"What do you think he's waiting for?"

It was Mr Furbelow who answered.

"I've thought about that a lot. I think he's waiting until there are more people like him. I think he became bored with people in his own time, galloping about and thumping each other, so he just put himself to sleep, until there were people he could talk to as equals."

"But there *can't* be anyone else like him," said Sally.

"Not yet, my dear, but one day, perhaps. You know, even after all this I still cannot believe in magic. Abracadabra and so on. I think he is a mutant."

"A what?"

"A mutant. I read about mutants in *Reader's Digest* which my late wife regularly subscribed to. It said that we all have, laid up inside us, a pattern of molecules which dictates what we are like – brown hair, blue eyes, that sort of thing, the features we inherit from our parents. And the patterns of molecules govern other things, it said, such as having two arms and two legs because we belong to the species *Homo sapiens*. A monkey is a monkey, with a tail, because of the pattern it inherits, and a fly is a fly, with faceted eyes, for the same reason. But apparently the pattern can be upset, by cosmic rays and atom bombs and such, and then you get a new kind of creature, with things about it which it didn't inherit from its parents and its species, and that's called a mutant."

"He was very big," said Sally, "and a funny rusty colour."

"Yes, and he had hair on his palms," said Geoffrey.

"It appears," said Mr Furbelow, "that most mutations are of that order, not mattering much one way or the other. Or else they are positively bad, such as not having a proper stomach, which means that the mutation dies out. But every now and then you get one which is really an improvement on the existing species, and then you get the process called evolution. I think I've got that right."

"It makes sense," said Geoffrey. "But we've got to think about how we're going to get out of here. He won't make any more food for us now. And we must decide what we're going to tell people when we do get out."

"But where did he get all that strength from?" said Sally. "Did he just have a bigger mind?"

"Perhaps," said Mr Furbelow. "But that would not be necessary. Did you know there is a great big bit of your mind you don't use at all? Nobody knows what it's for. I read that somewhere else, in another *Reader's Digest* I expect. I've wondered about all this a lot, you know, and I think perhaps that Man's next bit of evolution might be to learn to use that part of his brain, and that would give him powers he doesn't have now. And I cannot see why this jump should not occur from time to time in just one case but fail to start a new evolutionary chain. There have been other marvellous men besides Merlin, you know, if you read the stories. Perhaps some of them put themselves to sleep in the same way, and are waiting. Quite often they did not die – they just disappeared."

"I suppose," said Geoffrey, "it was the drugs which made him change England back to the Dark Ages. He was muddled, and wanted everything to be just as he was used to it. So he made everyone think machines were wicked, and forget how to work them."

"Do you think there were people who could change the weather in his day?" asked Sally. "Like you can, Jeff. He must have given you the power for some reason. Or perhaps there were just people who *said* they could, and he forgot. The drugs must have made it very confusing for him."

"Did you make the ice on the steps?" asked Mr Furbelow.

Geoffrey felt like a thief caught stealing, but nodded. Mr Furbelow was silent.

"You were justified," he said at last, "taking one thing with another. I thought about myself a lot in the night, when it seemed as if I were shortly to meet my Creator, and I discovered I had been blind and selfish. I tried to use him, you know. I tried to bind him to me with a habit-forming drug, so that he would have to do whatever I wished, like a genie in a bottle. But he was too strong for me, and I let him lie there in his cave, lost and sick, lost and sick. It was a sinful thing to do."

"Do you think England will start being ordinary again now?" said Sally.

"Yes," said Geoffrey. "And we really must decide what we are going to tell people – the General for instance. He'll start digging if we tell him Merlin's down there."

"General?" asked Mr Furbelow.

They explained, Geoffrey feeling more like a thief than ever. Mr Furbelow looked to and fro between them with sharp, glistening eyes.

"Goodness me," he said when they'd finished, "I never heard of anything more gallant in all my born days. Fancy their sending two children on a journey like that! And your carrying it off so! Do you mean that all the tale of the leech, your guardian, was an invention? It quite took me in, I must confess. Well, that *has* given me something to think about! Where were we?"

"Trying to decide what to tell the General," said Sally. "If we ever see him again. We must go before the wolves get hungry."

"Does everyone agree that we cannot tell the truth?" asked Mr Furbelow.

"Yes," said the children together.

"Then we must have a story," said Mr Furbelow.

"You had best work one out, Geoffrey, as you seem to have the knack."

"Simple and mysterious," said Sally. "Then we needn't pretend to understand it either."

"Have you got any horse-bait left, Sal?" said Geoffrey. "We've got to make a sort of litter for Mr Furbelow, and Maddox will have to carry it."

"I've got four bits. Two to get him up this side, and two down the other. Then we can go and get help."

They worked out the story while Geoffrey laboured and contrived: there had been no tower; the outer wall had been built by a big man with a beard, who had simply appeared one day, had sat down in front of Mr Furbelow's house and begun to meditate. He had never spoken a word, but the walls and the forest had grown round him, and the dogs had appeared. He had produced food out of thin air, and Mr Furbelow had felt constrained to wait on him. When the children came he had become enraged, wrecked the place and left, stalking off down the valley. That was all they knew.

"What about our clothes?" said Sally.

"We'll have to hide them," said Geoffrey. "And Mr Furbelow's medicines."

By some miracle the true well had not caved in. Sally

threw down it anything that spoilt the story, and then piled hundreds of cobblestones on top. They found some old clothes in chests of drawers in the cottage, mothy but wearable. The litter was a horrible problem, as most of the usable materials had been destroyed by fire or earthquake, and Geoffrey's ankle seemed to be hurting more and more. He was still hobbling round looking for lashings when the first jet came over, in the early afternoon.

It was very high, trailing a feathery line of vapour, and curved down out of sight beyond the hills. Ten minutes later it came back again, squealing down the valley at a few hundred feet. Sally waved a piece of the sheet which Geoffrey had been tearing into strips for the litter.

"He'll never see that," he said. The pain in his leg made him snarly. "We ought to try and make a smoke signal or something. Damp straw would do it."

"What can we light it with?" asked Sally.

"Oh hell. There might be some hot embers in the stables if you went and blew on them. You'd need something to scoop them up with, and..."

"He's coming back."

The jet came up the valley, even lower, flaps down,

engine full of the breathy roar of a machine not going its natural pace. Sally waved her sheet again. The wings tilted, and they could see the pilot's head, but so small that they couldn't be sure whether he was looking at them or not. The wings tilted the other way, then towards them again, then away.

"He's seen us," said Geoffrey. "He's waggling his wings."

The engine note rose to its proper whine, the nose tilted up and up until the plane was in a roaring vertical climb. It twisted its path again and whistled southwards. In less than a minute it was a dot over the southern horizon, trailing its streak of vapour.

"He was looking for *us*," said Sally.

"Yes," said Geoffrey. "We'd better stay. The litter wasn't going to work anyway."

"I hope they come soon," said Sally. "I'm hungry."

"I have just remembered," said Mr Furbelow, "there might be some tins in the cupboard in the kitchen. I haven't thought about them for five years. It was not the sort of thing he would have cared for."

There was some stewing steak and the trick with the embers worked, so they supped by a crackling fire in the open, like boy scouts, and slept under the stars.

Five helicopters came next morning, clattering along below a grey sky. A group of very tough-looking men jumped out of each machine and ran to the outer wall, where they trained their automatic weapons on the silent forest. Sally ran to warn them not to shoot the wolfhounds, who, restless with hunger, had gone hunting. One of the men aimed a gun at her as she talked, and she came back. Officers snapped orders, pointed out arcs of fire and doubled on to the next group. Three men stood in the middle of the courtyard in soldierly, commanding attitudes. They watched the activity for a while and then strolled over towards the cottage. The one in the middle was the General.

Geoffrey stood up, forgetting about his ankle. Ambushed by the pain he sprawled sideways, and stayed sitting as the three approached.

"Aha!" barked the General. "You do not obey the orders, young man. I say to you to make a *reconnaissance* (he pronounced the word the French way) and you defeat the enemy, you alone. That is no path to promotion. But this is the enemy, then?"

He pointed at Mr Furbelow. He seemed very pleased.

"No," said Geoffrey. "This is Mr Furbelow. He

broke his leg in the storm, and I tried to set it, but I think he ought to go to hospital as soon as possible."

"But the enemy?" snapped the General. He didn't seem interested in Mr Furbelow's leg.

"You mean the Necromancer," said Sally. "We only just saw him. He got angry when we came and he went away. Mr Furbelow can tell you far more about him than we can."

The General turned again to the old man on the ground, and stared at him in silence.

"How did you find out so quickly?" said Geoffrey.

One of the other men answered, an Englishman.

"Some bright boy in London came to and got in touch with Paris. He started an emergency generator at the FO and got a transmitter going. He hadn't a clue what was up, but the fact that he could work the machine at all encouraged us to send recce planes over. One of them spotted this place – we knew where you were heading for, of course – and here we are."

"Your Necromancer," said the General, "what is he?"

"Honestly, we don't know. He just sat and thought, Mr Furbelow says. He's been living with him for five years, but he's really much too tired to tell you anything now. Why don't you send him off to hospital, let him have a good rest, and then I'm sure he'll tell you all he knows?"

The Englishman spoke to the General in French, and the General grunted. The third man yelled an order, and two soldiers doubled over from one of the gun positions. They ran to the helicopters and ran back with a stretcher, on to which they quickly and tenderly eased Mr Furbelow. They must have practised the job a hundred times in their training.

"Where will you take him to?" said Sally.

"Paris," said the Englishman. "I expect you will be coming too, young lady."

"No thank you," said Sally. "I want to take Maddox to Weymouth as soon as Geoffrey's foot is better. If you could find us another horse we could ride down. And we'll need some money. The weatherman stole all ours."

The General grunted and sucked his lower lip over the little moustache.

"We had expected Mr Tinker to come to Paris to make a report," said the Englishman.

"Can you *make* me?" said Geoffrey. "I'll come if I have to, but I'd much rather not. We don't know anything, Sally and I. He went when we came. I'll write to Lord Montagu and explain about the Rolls. It was struck by lightning."

"You have already one horse?" barked the General.

Geoffrey pointed. Maddox was coming disconsolately round the courtyard looking for tender fragments of green weed and finding nothing. Some he'd eaten already and the rest the earthquake had obliterated. He was in a bitter temper, but stumped over towards the steps to see if Sally had any horse-bait left. The General was in the way. Maddox plodded towards him, snarling, then stopped. For a moment these two manifestations of absolute willpower gazed at each other; then the General laughed his yapping laugh and stepped aside.

"I am no more astonished that you have succeeded. With a weapon of that calibre."

The staff officers smiled obediently.

"Thomas," said the General, "envoyez des hommes chercher un bon cheval. Au delà de ces collines j'ai vu des petites fermes. We will talk to Mr Furbelow in Paris. Goodybye, M'sieu."

As the stretcher-bearers stooped to the poles Mr Furbelow turned to the children.

"I trust I shall see you again, my dears," he said. "I have much to thank you for."

"You are not alone," barked the General. "I too, England too, all have much to thank them for."

"The General will send you to Weymouth to stay with us," said Sally, "when your leg's better."

"I should appreciate that," said Mr Furbelow.

He was lifted into a helicopter which heaved itself rowdily off the ground, tilted its tail up and headed south. Five soldiers left to look for a second horse, but before they'd been gone ten minutes there was a noise of baying, followed by shots.

"Oh Lord," said Geoffrey. "I forgot about the wolves. I hope your men are all right."

The Englishman grinned. "Excellent practice," he said.

"This Mr Furbelow," snapped the General, "he will tell me the truth."

"Yes," said Geoffrey, "as much as he knows."

The General looked at him, sucking his moustache, for ages.

"Could somebody please look at my ankle?" said Geoffrey.

The third man shouted again, and one of the stretcher-men ran over. He had very strong, efficient hands, like tools designed to do a particular job, and he dressed Geoffrey's leg with ointments and a tight bandage. He spoke friendlily to Geoffrey in French, which the Englishman translated. Apparently there was only a mild strain, but the pain was caused by bruising. The General strutted off to listen to a radio in one of the helicopters. Watching him, Geoffrey realised why he had been so helpful about sending them back to Weymouth: it wouldn't do to have *two* heroes returning to France.

The soldiers began to lounge at their posts, but still kept a sharp watch on the forest, a ring of modern weapons directed outwards against an enemy who all the time lay in their midst, deep under the ridged rock, sleeping away the centuries.

They rode south three days later. The General had left six men to guard them, and together they went up the higher track. Half the oaks had fallen in the earthquake, and the ride was blocked every few yards. They saw no wolves. On the shoulder of the hill they said goodbye to their escort and went on alone.

The countryside was in a strange state. At almost every cottage gate there would be a woman standing to ask for news. On the first day, as they passed a group of farm buildings, they heard a wild burst of cheering and a rusty tractor chugged out into the open followed by a gang of excited men. Later they passed a car which had been pushed out into the road. Tools lay all round it and a man was sitting on the bank with his head between oily hands. The sky was busy with aeroplanes. They bought lunch at a store which was full of people who hadn't really come to buy anything, but only to swap stories and rumours. One woman told how she'd found herself suddenly wide awake in the middle of the night and had stretched out, for the first time in six years, to switch on the bedside light. Other people nodded. They'd done the same. Another woman came in brandishing a tin-opener, and was immediately besieged with requests to borrow it. There was an old man who blamed the whole thing on the atom bomb, and got into an angry argument with another old man who thought it had all been done by communists.

While they were eating their lunch it began to rain. They sheltered under a chestnut tree, but the rain didn't stop and drips began to seep between the broad leaves.

"Oh, Jeff, please stop it!"

Geoffrey felt under his jerkin for the gold robe, but didn't put it on. He realised, with a shock of regret, that now that the Necromancer lay asleep again, other things had settled back into place and his own powers were gone. Nothing that he could do would alter the steady march of weeping clouds, or call down perfect summers, or summon snow for Christmas. Not ever again.

And the English air would soon be reeking with petrol.

Printed by RR Donnelley at Glasgow, UK